.arla
ι Co

Period
v.meath

CHRISTMAS AT THE GINGER CAT CAFÉ

Jilted at the altar, Isla Marchant isn't feeling very festive this Christmas. So when her aunt and uncle invite her to run their café while they're away, she seizes the chance. Short one member of staff, Harry Anderton turns out to be the perfect solution when he pitches up in a campervan. Then Isla discovers that there are certain seasonal traditions she's expected to uphold in the café. With Harry by her side, can she contain her growing feelings and give the people around her the celebrations they deserve?

ZARA THORNE

CHRISTMAS AT
THE GINGER
CAT CAFÉ

Complete and Unabridged

LINFORD
Leicester

First published in Great Britain in 2018

First Linford Edition
published 2020

A catalogue record for this book is available
from the British Library.

ISBN 978–1–4448–4529–7

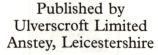

Published by
Ulverscroft Limited
Anstey, Leicestershire

Set by Words & Graphics Ltd.
Anstey, Leicestershire
Printed and bound in Great Britain by
TJ Books Limited, Padstow, Cornwall

This book is printed on acid-free paper

December 20th

Five days until Christmas

Isla Marchant sneezed for the fifth time that morning. The small Victorian terraced house in Albert Street was cosy and well-heated, and she didn't have a cold. Neither was she allergic to cats — at least she never had been before. She could only conclude that this new inconvenience was due to the sheer number of cats she'd found herself sharing the house with. Four, to be exact. Getting the vacuum out every day made no difference. Every corner of the house continued to harbour its own fairy ball of hair. The sofa, chairs and beds — Isla's bed in particular — all had a tell-tale smattering of fur of various colours.

'They need a good comb-through, that's all,' her mother advised when Isla rang her.

'Like I've got time for that. Anyway, I wouldn't know where to start.'

'Start at the top of the head and work down!'

Isla had the distinct impression her mother wasn't taking the problem seriously at all.

Aunt Jo and Uncle Lloyd hadn't said anything about combing the cats. Well, they'd just have to take their chance, as would Isla herself.

Whisky and Treacle, black-and-white and dark brown respectively, eyed her balefully from the top of the kitchen table, probably musing on her many shortcomings as a cat sitter. The others — a grey orange-eyed beauty called Sixpence, and Bentley, a big bruiser of a ginger cat — were no doubt upstairs, taking full advantage of Isla's bed, still warm from her recent occupancy.

The sneezing was a small price to pay for the relief of getting away from Nottingham for three whole months. She couldn't be more thankful to her aunt and uncle for understanding exactly what she needed, and trusting her to house-sit for them and run The Ginger Cat café while they were on a dream trip to Australia and New Zealand.

Tucked away in the rural Sussex backwater of Charnley Acre, the café keeping her busy, she might have some chance of forgetting about the wedding. The wedding that, in the end, wasn't a wedding at all. Who would want to stick around after they'd been left standing on the church porch, all done up in cream silk and lace, with the pews full of friends and relations? Apart from their mutual friends, the guests had all come from her side. Sam had no family — none he'd wanted to invite, anyway.

Isla's mother had said all along that having bridesmaids dressed in black was a bad omen. Looking back, Isla thought she might have had a point. Two of Isla's closest friends and a cousin from her father's side had made a dramatic trio in mid-calf, off-the-shoulder black dresses, offset with posies of cream and red roses to match Isla's bouquet.

But that was before they'd reached the church. Once it became apparent that the expected perfect day was missing one vital component — the groom — they'd looked more like three witches left over from a coven. Well, it was Halloween, a fact nobody had thought to mention when the colour choice had been made.

Bridesmaids in black might have been Isla's idea, but getting married in church certainly wasn't. In the end, though, it had been easier to let Mum have her way over the venue. Neither Isla's father nor Sam had been bothered what kind of wedding it was, as long as the women were happy.

In time, the nightmare non-wedding might fade from her mind. If only the same applied to Sam, she'd be sailing in safer waters.

Like that was ever going to happen.

Isla picked a white hair off the edge of her bowl of cereal and decided she didn't fancy it anymore. Five minutes later, warmly dressed in boots, navy-blue coat and a yellow knitted hat, she set out into the frosty morning.

★　★　★

At number two Honeypot Square, Molly Spinks rolled out of bed before her mother woke up the whole neighbourhood with yelling up the stairs. She wished it was Saturday — at least she got an extra half-hour's lie-in then. During the week, Molly worked at The Ginger Cat café. On Saturdays, she worked at Charnley Acre's one and only hair salon. She was only allowed to wash hair, sweep it up off the floor and make the tea, but she watched the stylists at work and dreamed of the day when she'd be a stylist herself, not in a village at the back end of nowhere, but in London, or New York, or Paris.

She'd applied to go to college to study hair and beauty, but even if by some miracle she got in, she wouldn't start until next September. Meanwhile, she had to content herself with her Saturday job at the salon, and working in The Ginger Cat.

Molly enjoyed her job at the café, though. At least she got to talk to the customers on an equal footing and not as the lowliest of juniors. Sometimes in the salon, she'd be standing there with the broom in her hand, feeling exactly like Cinderella.

She'd said that to Jake Harrison one night in October, when they'd been to the cinema at Cliffhaven, the nearest sizeable town, with other friends from the village. He'd laughed, not in a mocking way but sympathetically. And then he'd drawn her to one side in the shadows of the square and kissed her. A real kiss, on the mouth. It hadn't been her first kiss ever — she had been sixteen at the time, seventeen now — but her first with Jake, and therefore the one she would always treasure.

Jake lived conveniently close, on the other side of Honeypot Square. They'd walked home together several times since that night, but the kiss had never been repeated.

Molly's ambition to become Jake's girl-friend trumped her ambition to become a top hair stylist ten times over. She'd never been out with him on her own, on a proper date, and yet he must like her a bit, otherwise he'd never have kissed her in the first place.

Molly thought about this as she dallied over her tea and cereal in the kitchen. When did she ever *not* think about it? Perhaps she should do what other girls did and ask Jake out on a date. Girls didn't have to wait around anymore. But supposing he said no? He might even laugh at her. She'd be totally humiliated, and things between them would be awkward forevermore, whereas at least now they were friends. She hadn't ruled it out, though. She'd wait and see how she felt after Christmas.

Let's wait until after Christmas. Everyone said that, didn't they, about all kinds of things? *We'll just get Christmas out of the way, and then* . . . As if it made any difference which side of Christmas you did this or that. It was just an excuse, really. What was that word? Pro-crastination, that was it.

Mum was in the other room, hoover-ing up pine needles again. Why they didn't have a fake Christmas tree, Molly had no idea. You could get marvellous ones now, some with lights already on them, and snow on the branches and everything. The catalogues were full of them. But Mum wouldn't have it. It had to be a real tree or nothing. Molly had the feeling this idea had come from her dad, originally — he'd died when Molly was nine — and the real Christmas tree was Mum's way of keeping a special memory alive, although she never said, and Molly didn't ask.

This year, Christmas had become a delicate subject in the Spinks household of two, and it was nothing to do with Christmas trees. Molly had been expect-ing to go to Nan's, as usual. Nan lived quite close, halfway between Charnley Acre and Cliffhaven. They always went there on Christmas morning in a taxi and came back the same night. But no.

This year, apparently they were going to Auntie Jean's in Brighton on Christmas Eve and staying right through until the day after Boxing Day, which meant that Molly would miss out on Sarah Martin's Christmas Eve party.

Sarah lived in one of the big houses behind St Luke's church. Whenever she had a party, which was quite often, her parents stayed around in the background to fend off any gatecrashers and curb the alcohol, but otherwise didn't interfere. There'd be great food and music and dancing — dancing in a tongue-in-cheek kind of way for those who thought they were too cool to dance. Everyone would be there, absolutely everyone, and that included Jake. If he walked home with her — and there was no reason why he shouldn't — he might kiss her again, because it was Christmas if nothing else.

On the other hand, he might not. But Molly's natural optimism didn't allow her to entertain that possibility for long.

Her mother couldn't see the problem.

They'd be having a good time at Auntie Jean's, wouldn't they? She and Uncle Alan always had a houseful at Christmas. What on earth was Molly worrying about a silly party for?

She might as well have run a stake through Molly's heart.

Molly looked at the clock and leapt up from the table. Moments later, she was haring across the square, coat flapping open and blonde ponytail swinging.

★　★　★

At Malt Cottage, a tiny dwelling in the high street squeezed in between the butcher's and the art and craft shop, Horace Penfold threw two eggs into the frying pan already slick with yesterday's fat. Both yolks split straight away but Horace wasn't bothered. The eggs would slide down nicely with several thick slices of toast and a second mug of tea. He smiled with satisfaction as blue smoke rose to the already tainted ceiling. If there was one thing the perishing cold weather demanded, it was a proper break-fast. Setting out on an empty stomach did you no good at all.

Setting his plate down on the rickety oilcloth-covered table, Horace remembered his teeth and stomped upstairs to fetch them from the glass beside the bed. Downstairs again, tucking into his eggs with relish, he allowed himself a few moments' reflection on last evening at The Goose and Feather. It had been a busy night — weren't they all so close to Christmas? Damn tree got in the way, as usual. People would stand their empty glasses down in the corner where it stood, meaning Horace had to bend and scrabble about in the half-dark to gather them up and risk getting poked in the eye by lethal branches. Plus, he must have been up and down to that cellar nigh on twenty times last night.

The landlord was a good sort though. Always saw Horace right with his fair share of the tips. Yes, he was lucky there, having a job at The Goose, his spiritual home, and only yards from his own front door. Not many could boast of such convenience.

The Ginger Cat, Horace's daytime place of work, was also only yards away, on the opposite side of the high street. It wasn't bad there either. Jo and Lloyd ran the place like clockwork, which Horace greatly admired. This new person, Isla, a niece or something, seemed far too young for such responsibility. She seemed to be shaping up well enough, though, despite half her hair being purple. Once Horace had given her a few pointers on how to run the place, based on the wealth of experience he'd gained from years of working at the Savoy in London, she'd settled in well enough.

His breakfast finished, Horace dropped his greasy plate in the yellowing sink and slopped the dregs of his tea on top. He'd wash up tonight, with his supper things. No point in wasting hot water.

Walking through to his little sitting room, Horace tweaked the curtains apart to check on the weather. A full ashtray stood on the windowsill. He'd see to that tonight as well. Or on Sunday when he had more time. A movement in the street caught his eye, along with a flash of bright red. Horace quickly tweaked the curtains together again. He could still see her through the gap: Olive Cowstick. Every time their paths crossed she made a beeline for him. Wanting to know if he'd seen this or that on telly, asking what he'd got for his dinner, how he was coping with the cold weather — every damn thing about him. She'd knocked on his door once and presented him with a homemade fruit cake. Just like that, out of the blue. Another time it was lemon and poppyseed. The seeds had stuck in his teeth and got under his plate. He had to say Olive was a dab hand at baking, but why she'd singled him out to receive this bounty he had no idea.

She would keep turning up in The Ginger Cat, too. Angling things so it was Horace who got to serve her and nobody else.

What was her game? he wondered.

13

Olive's husband, Fred, had passed, what would it be? Two years ago? Three? Word had it that she used to boss him about something shocking — bossed him into an early grave, Horace shouldn't wonder. Well, if she thought she could do the same to him, she could think again. Horace might be widowed himself, but his Maureen had been the only girl for him. Oh, she'd kept him in order all right, or thought she had. But that was women's way, and who'd argue about that?

Horace's home life now was female-free, which in his opinion was a very satisfactory state of affairs.

Shuffling into his shoes and throwing on his coat, he checked his pocket for his ciggies and lighter before slamming the door of Malt Cottage and setting off across the street.

★ ★ ★

It was three o'clock in the afternoon by the time Harry Anderton drove the

14

borrowed campervan over the brow of the hill and down the other side into Charnley Acre. As he nosed the van along the high street, he couldn't help but notice how the eyes of everyone passing by were following his progress with interest. As well they might, as Harry had no idea where he was going.

It seemed sensible to get out of the high street. Clearly he couldn't park here. The street was narrow and had a number of tight turnings leading to the side streets. Any attempt at tricky manoeuvres would be bound to land him in trouble. Getting himself from Oxford to Sussex via the motorways and main roads hadn't been a problem. This dinky little village was another matter entirely.

Wondering for the umpteenth time why he'd chosen this particular spot in which to start his life afresh, Harry drove on, keeping his eye out for wider spaces more conducive to a first-time campervan driver. He'd not even thought about where to park overnight.

Right now, his priority was finding a quiet place to stop and take a break.

Towards the end of the high street, he noticed a library and a small school on his left; to his right, a reassuringly modern-looking medical centre. A little further on, he was able to turn off the high street and into a road of a decent width. *Albert Street*, read the sign. On one side sat a neat terrace of Victorian villas. On the other, a park stretched away to a bank of trees. There were paths running across the park leading to a children's playground in the centre, but they were clearly not designed for vehicles, even if he could have got the van through the gap between the entrance posts.

But Albert Street itself was wide enough for him to park without obstructing the pavement by more than a foot and, best of all, it seemed deserted, apart from a large ginger cat surveying the wintry world from the top of a wooden post.

The day was already closing in by the

time Harry had taken a brief nap on the surprisingly comfortable banquette arrangement before working out how to make a cup of tea. Thankfully, he'd stocked up with the basics before he'd made the journey. He didn't fancy trekking to the shop he'd seen in the high street. He'd even worked out how to switch on the tiny heater, which was surprisingly effective once he'd got it positioned correctly.

Yes, he'd be fine in his miniature home, for the time being, anyway. All he had to do was wait it out until after Christmas, when his rental cottage would be available. He could have stayed in Oxford for longer and avoided the winter camping set-up entirely, but once his plans were set and the loose threads of his old life if not exactly tied up but roughly bundled, he'd thought about nothing else but getting on the road and away.

After a while, he stepped down from the van, locked it up and took a walk in the park to stretch his legs. The expanse of green already felt crisp underfoot and across the far side, the tops of the bare trees were cloaked in mist. The park was empty apart from a man walking a spaniel. The dog-walker nodded at Harry as they passed one another, but neither spoke.

As he strolled in a circular route, Harry checked his phone, although he'd not long ago looked at it. It was habit more than anything, a hangover from that gut-wrenching period of his life when every phone call or text message brought a fresh rush of hope that it was Claudia, getting in touch to tell him she'd made a huge mistake and would he please come home so that they could sort it out. Of course, she never had.

Her number was still in his list of contacts. He looked at it now with surprise, as if he thought he'd deleted it while, deep down he knew that he hadn't. Even now, months later, he still smarted from the pain of her deception.

Back inside the van, Harry took his tablet from his luggage, gave it a boost with the charger, and set about searching for campsites. It didn't take him long to discover that there weren't any, unless he wanted to travel further westwards to Brighton, or east to Eastbourne or Hastings. He didn't. At least, not tonight.

He studied the street through the windscreen. The street-lamps had come on, spooling apricot discs onto the pavements, and the houses were beginning to show lights in the windows. He'd seen one or two people coming and going, including a woman who'd let herself into the house opposite his van. Medium height, dark-haired, she'd been wearing a dark-coloured coat over jeans, with boots, and a yellow knitted hat which cast a cheerful spot of colour in the grey gloom of the dying afternoon. The ginger cat had followed her indoors.

Seeing the girl brought a pang of self-pity, the first since he'd set out from Oxford this morning. *Enough of that*. He'd have another rest and sort out his sleeping quarters for tonight before walking to that pub he'd seen in the high street, The Goose and Feather. The sign said they did food. And then he'd come back and settle down for the night, exactly where he was. It was probably against some byelaw or other to set up camp by the side of the road, but he wasn't in anyone's way and it seemed unlikely he'd be disturbed on a dark December night.

December 21st
The Winter Solstice

Four days until Christmas

Isla wouldn't have given the campervan a second thought had she not looked out late last night and seen the light behind the curtains in its windows. A campervan parked innocuously overnight was one thing; one with somebody living in it, quite another. Who would be camping in the middle of a freezing December? And why in the village and not on a proper site, or at least in a field somewhere?

Treacle and Bentley, who'd been watching out of the window from the back of the armchair, swivelled their heads round at the sound of her voice, which was when she realised she'd asked the questions out loud.

21

'Okay, I'm talking to cats. I've finally cracked.'

She kneeled up on the chair and peered out of the window between the cats, scrutinising the campervan for further signs of life. All was quiet and still. But that wasn't the point. She'd been left in charge of this house; she alone was responsible for its safekeeping. And she was out all day, every day. It wouldn't take a genius to work that out if they were watching the house. Somebody living in a campervan in winter, just before Christmas, too, obviously had nowhere else to go. That in itself was reason to be suspicious.

Isla threw on her coat, grabbed her door key and darted across the road before her courage failed her. The campervan door opened onto the pavement side. She ran round and rapped on the door, then took a few steps back, her arms folded around herself. After a moment, the door was opened halfway by a man whom she guessed to be in his early thirties, the same as she was.

'Hello,' he said, opening the door fully and turning on an appealing smile. 'Can I help?'

'Oh, I . . . '

He wasn't all what she'd expected, although she wasn't sure now what she had been expecting. She blushed a bit when she realised she was openly looking him up and down. She couldn't help it. He seemed to be wearing two pairs of trousers. The denim waistband of his jeans sat an inch above that of the khaki cords on top of them. His black jumper showed a certain amount of strain, unsurprising, as beneath it a red one was visible and a shirt below that. And either he had very large feet or there was a second pair of heavy-duty grey socks, the sort for wearing under wellington boots, underneath the top ones. A grey beanie hat topped off this ensemble.

His eyes followed hers. 'Yes, sorry. I must look like a tramp. I wasn't expecting visitors.'

He whipped off the hat, revealing dark brown hair in a short-cropped style, accentuating strong, even features and candid grey-blue eyes. He didn't look like a vagrant, despite the odd layers of clothing. But appearances could be deceptive.

Isla conjured up a smile. 'No, *I'm* sorry. I didn't mean to stare. It's just . . . ' *Just what?* 'It's just that I saw your campervan last night, and when it was still here this morning I thought I'd better investigate. I'm housesitting, you see. Across the road.' She pointed.

'Yes, I saw you come home yesterday afternoon.'

So he *had* been watching the house. And all the other houses in the street, no doubt.

'Look,' Isla said, 'you can't stay here. This is a residential area, not a camp-site.'

'I realise that. Look, why don't you come in?' He held the door wider. 'I can't promise it's any warmer in than it is out. In fact, if last night was anything to go by, I'd say it definitely isn't. There is a small heater which does something but not enough, as it turns out. But come in anyway.'

'No, thank you. I've got to get to work. I just wondered how long you intended to stay here, if it's not too personal a question?'

'I've been wondering that myself.'

His gaze dropped momentarily. Something inside Isla gave way. 'Are you in some kind of trouble?'

'Trouble? No, no. I'm between lodgings, that's all. This is temporary, until my new place is ready.'

'That's something, I suppose.' Isla wondered where his new place was. Not that she cared.

'I'll be driving out later to find a proper campsite. This one isn't exactly bristling with facilities.' He gave a little laugh. 'Don't worry, I'll be gone by the time you get home.'

'But it's freezing. You can't camp out in this, even on a site.'

'I'll be fine. I might lose a few toes to frostbite but there you go.'

The sparkle in his eye told her that

was a pure joke, not a play for sympathy. 'Well, I can't stand here all day. Good luck!' She crossed the road and went indoors.

The house phone was ringing. She hoped it wasn't her mother fancying an early-morning chat. Talking to Campervan Man had already put her behind, and the cats hadn't even been fed yet. She picked up the phone.

'Isla? It's Maggie. I'm ever so sorry but I can't come in today.'

Isla drew in a breath and looked up at the ceiling. The Ginger Cat was frantically busy and there wouldn't be any let-up until after Christmas; Jo and Lloyd had warned her of that. Maggie, a cheerful woman in her sixties with a seemingly endless store of energy, was the most reliable and efficient member of the team. Not only did she wait on tables at the speed of light, she did most of the cooking as well.

'That's okay, Mags. We'll manage.' Isla effected a lightness she didn't feel. 'See you tomorrow.'

'Ah, no . . . '

'No?'

'I'm down at Cliffhaven General, in A&E. I got up in the night to spend a penny, like you do, and didn't put the light on. Went straight down the stairs, top to bottom! Don wanted to send for the ambulance but I said no, you drive me. So he did, and here we sits like birds in the wilderness.'

'You're still waiting to be seen?'

'Waiting to get plastered or whatever it is they do now. I've been to X-ray and they say my ankle's gone. I'm ever so sorry to let you down, lovely. This'll take a while to mend.'

'Of course it will. Maggie, I'm so sorry, and please don't worry about the café. We'll be fine. Make sure Don gives you plenty of TLC.'

When she'd put the phone down, Isla stood for a moment, her hands to her mouth. So now it was just her, Horace — as slow as a boat and miserable with it — and Molly, slapdash at the best of times and now even worse because she was daydreaming over some boy or other. The afternoons would pose an extra problem because Horace finished work after the lunchtime rush. She couldn't ask him to do extra hours because of his evening job at the pub. It was a miracle he kept both jobs going as it was; he must be eighty at least.

Well, she'd just have to manage. What choice was there? The chances of finding somebody to fill in at such short notice, four days before Christmas, were as remote as Santa's workshop at the North Pole.

The cats were winding themselves round her legs, meowing and pointedly licking the bits stuck to the floor around the empty food bowls.

'Okay, you lot next. There's no need to go on.'

The cats sorted — her own breakfast would have to wait until she got to the café — Isla ran upstairs for her bag and the other things she needed for the day. Glancing out of the bedroom window, she saw the campervan, glowing white in the early-morning murk. Okay, she'd be taking a big risk and he'd probably say no anyway. In fact she hoped he would. This was the stupidest idea she'd had since she'd bothered to turn up at her own wedding.

Harry — that was his name — clearly thought the opposite.

'I can't believe you're offering me a room, Isla,' he said, blowing on his hands as he followed her back across the street. 'You don't know me from Adam. I'll pay you rent, of course.'

'We'll talk about that later. I don't suppose you've got any catering experience?'

'I served breakfasts at a hotel when I was a student and I've worked in pubs. That was quite a while ago now. Why?'

* * *

She'd given Harry directions to The Ginger Cat. It was only eight minutes from Albert Street, bang in the middle of the high street, so he couldn't miss it.

Even so, Isla's eyes kept darting to the door in case she'd misjudged him entirely and he was at this moment zipping across Sussex in the campervan with half the contents of the house on board.

But no, here he was, pushing tentatively at the glass door, and smiling as he caught her eye.

Shrugging out of his coat, he came round to her side of the service counter. He looked a lot slimmer without the extra layers of clothes, and his face was smooth from a recent shave.

'Harry Anderton, reporting for duty.' He gave a mock salute. 'That shower hit the spot. Thanks, Isla.'

Two heads immediately turned in their direction. Horace's jaw dropped open, revealing a mouthful of nicotine-stained NHS gnashers, and Molly sniggered. After a quick round of introductions, Isla set Harry to work filling the trays inside the glass counter with the day's selection of cakes, pastries, sausage rolls and scones. Luckily, Maggie had filled the freezer with the different kinds of scones last week. Other cakes had been made by Jo and similarly frozen, to be defrosted and decorated as needed. The rest of the cakes, the sausage rolls, and items like the lunchtime quiches, were bought in.

By ten o'clock, all the tables in The Ginger Cat were occupied by at least one person. Harry's beaming greeting to the customers was impressive, Isla had to admit, as was the way he handled the orders and brought them swiftly to the counter.

'Leave the coffees to us for now,' she said. 'The machine's a bit tricky if you're not familiar.'

'The cats aren't easy either,' Molly added, coming up alongside Harry.

'Cats?' He looked around the floor, making Molly giggle again. She was doing a lot of that this morning, but at least it was an improvement on the mournful-eyed lovesick look she usually displayed.

'On top of the coffee. You use the stencils to make them, but only for the coffees that have chocolate on top if the customer wants it.'

'Right, I see,' Harry said, looking slightly confused.

He watched as Molly merrily fluffed chocolate powder through the stencil onto somebody's cappuccino, and all over the counter while she was about it. The cat was missing its tail.

'If they don't want chocolate, you swirl the foam in a star shape as it goes through the tube, because it's Christmas. When it's not Christmas, you do a leaf or a flower.'

Molly's rapid demonstration with a medium latte resulted in something that looked more like a dog's turd than a star. Isla closed her eyes as the girl weaved perilously between the tables to deliver the coffees to their destination.

'It is very cat-orientated, isn't it?' Harry said to Isla, gazing around at the cats scampering around the red-painted walls, over the tablecloths and the crockery. 'As well as very Christmassy.' He pulled a face. It only lasted a second but Isla didn't miss it.

'You don't like Christmas,' she observed casually, watching closely for Harry's reaction.

'It's not that. I'm not doing Christmas this year.'

His closed-up expression warned Isla against questioning. 'Neither am I,' she said. 'The twenty-fifth will be an entirely Christmas-free zone. I'm planning on spending the day at home, catching up with the café accounts and not thinking about Christmas at all. If you're still around, that's the way it will be. You should know that.'

'Suits me,' Harry said, and turned his attention to the toaster.

He wasn't wrong about the café being Christmassy. Before they left, Jo and Lloyd had put up the tree and decorated it with vintage-style baubles and ornaments. Multi-coloured fairy lights twinkled along the shelf edges, and folded paper lanterns swung from the ceiling beams. There were sprigs of real holly in the cat-decorated jugs on the windowsills. Fake ivy, sparkling with fake frost, had been wound around everything it was possible to wind it round. A sign saying *Peace and Joy* hung on the wall behind the service counter.

There was no getting away from Christmas in The Ginger Cat. Isla constantly reminded herself it was for the customers' benefit, not hers. The trouble was, everyone was talking about Christmas as well, all other conversational topics having been forgotten. Isla would smile and nod while she listened to her female customers crowing triumphantly over some much-hyped toy of the year which they'd managed to procure, with great difficulty, for their child or grandchild. Food was high on the conversational agenda, too, as people wondered out loud if they'd put enough brandy in the cake, whether they should jazz up the sprouts with chestnuts or keep them plain for the grans and grandads, and what on earth they could cook for the niece who'd turned vegetarian overnight.

Isla's mother was in full festive swing,

too; Isla knew that from experience and the odd reference that had come up in their phone chats. Mum couldn't help it — Christmas at home in Nottingham was a traditional affair, and much planning went into it. But each time her mother mentioned anything remotely to do with the festivities, it was obvious from the pause that followed that she wished she could retract her words. This would have been Isla and Sam's first Christmas as a married couple. A special time, a time to make memories.

And now here Isla was, doing her best to pretend it wasn't happening.

Sam had flown to New York to spend Christmas with his sister: she'd been told that by several friends, including the bridesmaids-in-black. They all meant well, of course. In their eyes, they were passing on valuable information. Isla wanted to reply that she couldn't care less what Sam was doing for Christmas. But she hadn't because she wasn't sure it was true. All she knew was that every time she heard his name, it was like a red-hot skewer passing through her.

She kept a surreptitious eye on Harry throughout the day. He was an asset, she decided early on. Easy-going with the customers, fast and efficient with the food preparation and service, even if he had managed to set off the smoke alarm twice by switching up the toaster too high.

Molly was clearly impressed, if not a tiny bit besotted, as Harry gently joshed with her. Horace took no notice of Harry whatsoever. He flogged around the café in his usual fashion, raising his eyes if anyone hesitated a second too long over the menu. But Horace was Horace; he was as much a part of the village as the war memorial, and as such was treated with respect and a great deal of fondness by the regular customers.

It was only when Isla went out to the bins in the back yard and found Horace having his pre-lunch ciggie that the old man made mention of the newest member of staff.

'Where d'you find 'im, then? The

young fellow-me-lad?' Horace nodded towards the door as he flicked ash perilously near the paper recycling bin.

'Harry? I picked him up in the street,' Isla replied airily. 'He's a great help, isn't he?'

'Could do worse, I s'pose.'

And that, coming from Horace, was praise indeed.

★   ★   ★

Molly's feet were killing her due to the fact that she'd been run off them all day. It was only to be expected though, with Christmas round the corner.

The new guy, Harry, had soon fallen into step. He was ace with the serving, but not quite so much the cooking and stuff, even simple things like bashed-up avocado on sourdough toast, neither of which Molly could stomach at any price, on trend or not. He'd burnt the toast and left bits of skin in the avocado which Molly had helped to pick out to save him starting all over again. The customers liked him, though, especially the women. Molly had noticed that. She couldn't say she blamed them.

Isla had never said where she got Harry from and it seemed rude to ask. Perhaps he was a mate of hers, although she'd not been in the village long enough to make many new friends. An old boyfriend from home, perhaps? Someone she'd got in touch with because, with Maggie gone, they were desperate? Not that you'd have to be desperate to call on somebody as good-looking as Harry.

No, it couldn't be that. Isla came from up north somewhere. Nottingham, that was it. This Harry bloke must have been around already to have filled in at The Ginger Cat at a moment's notice. Anyway, they didn't act like they knew each other that well. They were quite pally by the time the café closed, though. Molly had noticed that, too.

As she walked home just after five, the cold nipping painfully at her ears, it seemed like night-time already. It was the shortest day of the year: the winter solstice. Mum had been chatting away about it this morning, trying to get Molly chatting, too, and lift her out of her mood. It hadn't worked. Mum had let out a big sigh, given up trying to jolly her along, and had gone off to her job at the florist's.

Nothing had changed. They were still going to Auntie Jean's on Christmas Eve. Molly was still going to miss Sarah's party and the possibility of getting together with Jake Harrison. With this depressing thought in her head, she took the turning off the high street that let to Honeypot Square and there, just up ahead but walking quite fast, was Jake. He must have got off the bus she'd seen as she'd left The Ginger Cat. Jake was eighteen; he worked at some sort of engineering place down at Cliffhaven.

Molly increased her pace and called out to him. For a moment she thought he hadn't heard, and then he stopped at the corner of Honeypot Square and turned round.

'Hey, Moll. How you doin'?'

Molly hurried to catch up, which made her embarrassingly out of breath.

'I'm good, thanks. You?' She stood beside him, hoping he'd stay and chat for a bit before he went home, but he began to walk on.

'Yep. Fine.'

Was that it? End of conversation? Molly grappled for something interesting to say that would detain him. They were nearly at Jake's house now. She should have crossed the square to her house before, but who knew when she'd have the chance to talk to him again?

'What are you doing for Christmas?' It was all she could think of.

Jake glanced down at his feet. 'Dunno yet. It's all gone a bit skywards.'

'Has it?' Molly said. What had gone skywards?

'Yep. Have to wait and see.'

'There's not a lot of time left to wait and see.'

'No, well . . . ' They were outside Jake's house now. A rectangle of light fell from the window across the small front garden. 'Better go in. See you, Mollykins.'

'Yep. See you around.'

Molly trailed home across the square. She looked back once but Jake had gone indoors, and the curtains had been drawn across the window, casting the house into deep shadow.

She liked him *so* much! More than she'd ever liked a boy before. Why couldn't he just like her back? Why did life have to be so flippin' difficult?

★   ★   ★

Horace stood in his kitchen and peered into the huge cast-iron pot in which he cooked his dinner most nights. He poked the cold, congealed contents with a dented aluminium spoon and located several pieces of rabbit. Satisfied that there was enough of the meat left to make tonight's meal, he went to the larder and brought out an ancient cardboard box which had once contained boxes of washing powder and now held his supply of fresh vegetables. Fresh, according to Horace, meant not frozen or tinned. It did not necessarily mean they were recent purchases. He picked over the contents of the box. Some of the spuds had gone a bit soft and the carrots and turnips were wrinkly, but perfectly good to eat all the same.

Waste not, want not, as his Maureen used to say.

She always made a good stew, did Maureen. Rib-sticking grub that hit the spot. Horace's stew-making skills weren't quite up to her standards, but he'd learned enough by practising and remembering how she did it to come up with a decent enough dinner. Once you'd learned, what did it matter if you had the same thing nearly every night? The stew, with rabbit or a nice bit of chuck steak, cut small, did him fine. If he fancied a change from stew, he'd put a tin of baked beans alongside a wedge of pork pie, or pay a visit to the fish and chip van that came to the village once a week. There was one of those Chinese takeaway places in the village, but Horace couldn't abide 'foreign muck'. He liked to know what he was eating.

He had just begun peeling and chopping carrots to bulk out tonight's stew when he heard the door knocker. Cursing under his breath, he went and opened it without thinking twice and almost shut it again when he saw who his visitor was.

Olive Cowstick stepped forward, looking as sturdy as a pillar-box in her red coat. She beamed at him.

'Saw you was at home by the light.'

'Oh, did you now? You couldn't have seen it from your place. It's round the corner.'

'Well, I'm here now.' Olive lifted a basket covered by a tea cloth. 'I brought you some supper. Had it going spare, so I thought, why not take it round to Horace and give him a treat?'

'You know what thought did. As it goes, my supper's well on the way.'

Olive's gaze travelled downwards.

Horace's followed, and he realised he was holding the vegetable knife, the blade pointing menacingly towards Olive.

'Peeling veg,' he said, feeling the shreds of desperation.

Was the woman going to stand on his doorstep all night, letting in the cold air?

Olive nodded knowingly. 'Take a look, shall I?'

Horace was just about to say he was perfectly capable of peeling a few carrots without interference when Olive launched herself into his hallway, forcing Horace to step aside. Raising his eyes, he closed the door behind her.

She marched straight through to the kitchen without invitation, lifted the lid on the iron pot, and wrinkled her nose at the contents.

'I think we can do better than this. A *lot* better.' She plonked the basket down on the table.

'Now, look here,' Horace said, still wielding the knife. 'It's not right to come barging into a person's house without

44

so much as a by-your-leave. A man needs his privacy.'

'You working tonight, at The Goose?'

'Not tonight, no.'

'Good. Then you've got time to enjoy a right good dinner.' Olive whipped the tea cloth off the basket. 'Gammon. I bought it for meself but it's too much for one.'

The joint of glistening pinkish-brown meat sprinkled with herbs sent out a fragrance that had Horace's taste buds doing the tango. Next to the meat were two lidded ice-cream cartons. Olive slid the lids aside, allowing Horace a view of the contents.

'Mashed potato, done with plenty of pepper and butter. Can't have gammon without mash. And cabbage, nice bit of Savoy. All cooked, just wants warming up. I even brought the mustard.' Olive held up a half-full jar of Coleman's.

Horace stared at the basket. He hadn't had gammon since Maureen had passed, and then it was only on high days and holidays.

'Tempted, Horace?' Olive tipped her head on one side, widening her eyes coquettishly.

Somehow, she'd taken off her red coat without him noticing. Her ample chest, clad in pea-green wool with a rope of pearls dangling suggestively mid-bosom, took up much of the space between them. Horace reeled backwards and collided with the edge of the sink.

'That could do with a good scouring,' Olive said, peering over his shoulder. 'I've got some stuff that'll shift the stains. I'll bring it round sometime, give it a good going over. I'll give your stove some elbow grease while I'm at it.'

Horace's stomach lowered itself in despair. But he wasn't done for yet. 'I do me cleaning on Sundays. I am a working man, you know.'

'I know you are, Horace. Not easy to find the time for housework, is it?'

She nodded sympathetically. If she thought she was going to get her feet under his table by being all soft with him, she'd got another think coming.

'So, what's it to be?' She pointed at the basket. 'Best boiled gammon, or whatever muck you've got in that pot?'

Horace thought for a moment. 'Go on, then. You warm up the grub. I'll set two places.'

Well, what was he supposed to do? His stomach was rumbling, and that gammon smelt so good.

Horace had to admit it made a pleasant change to have some company at his evening meal, even if it was Olive Cowstick. She didn't outstay her welcome, either.

He'd got out the plates and lit the oven but otherwise left her to get on with warming up the food while he'd generously poured two glasses of Guinness.

'Are you trying to get me tiddly, Horace Penfold?' she'd said, her blue eyes twinkling at him as she licked froth off her top lip.

He'd had to chuckle at the preposterousness of this idea. From then on, he'd let his guard down and they'd had a bit of a chinwag about this and that. But after the dinner was eaten and the little old clock on the front room mantelpiece wheezily struck half past eight, Horace had faked a yawn. Olive wasn't fooled but she'd taken the hint.

'See you tomorrow in The Ginger Cat,' she'd said, stepping out of his front door into the icy night, the basket over her arm. She'd made it sound more like a threat than a promise.

He might have let her have her way tonight, Horace told himself, as he looked at plates Olive had washed up and left to drain, but that didn't give her leave to foist herself on him any time she felt like it. Oh no, from now on he'd have to watch Olive Cowstick like a barn owl watching a mouse.

★   ★   ★

As Harry changed the tablecloths in the café, ready for the morning, he ran over the events of the day in his mind. This morning he'd woken, freezing and miserable, in that tin can of a campervan, wondering how he was going to pass the time until it was time to try and sleep again. And now, eight hours later, he had a temporary job and a place to stay, under a proper roof. He'd not been looking for or expecting to find either of these things, and he'd have managed without, but he couldn't help but thank the lucky star that had decided to shine on him.

A lucky star by the name of Isla Marchant.

She'd asked him no questions, simply taken him at face value. How refreshing that was. Refreshing, but unwise in the extreme — he'd taken Claudia at face value, and look how that had turned out.

He'd worked his way through the day, chatting politely to the customers and trying not to make too many mistakes with the orders in case he let Isla down. The café had been so busy that he hadn't checked his phone once or given any thought to the disastrous circumstances which had led to him changing his life. Or beginning to — he wasn't there yet, by any means, but there was a definite light flickering on the horizon.

There'd been one flaw in the smooth running of his day. He'd been clearing one of the window tables when two women, one pushing a baby buggy, had stopped outside to peruse the menu. Silently, Harry had urged them to walk right on by, but the door had been pushed open, forcing him to do his bit for customer relations and hold the door wide enough for the women, possibly mother and daughter, to enter with the buggy. Horace had been on a break out the back, Isla lining up coffees at the counter, while Molly flitted from counter to tables with her tray. It had been left to him to attend to the women, who'd settled at the table he'd just cleared.

The hood of the buggy had come down, and a pink-cheeked tot in a Peppa Pig hat had favoured Harry with a dribbly smile as he took the women's orders for lunch. The pencil had frozen in his hand as his brain fought away the image of another child, the one he had never set eyes on except in his imagination. And then the elder of the two women had asked him a question about omelette fillings and he'd pulled himself together and hauled himself out of the familiar downward spiral.

Horace had left after lunch. Molly had gone now, too, leaving just him and Isla. She came over as he spread the last table with its clean cloth and replaced the condiment basket.

'We're done. Come on, let's get home.' She handed him his coat and scarf.

As they walked back along the high street, they passed the pub where he'd enjoyed a very acceptable meal last night, and Harry felt suddenly apprehensive about the prospect of the evening ahead. He'd not had time to think about food for tonight, and he could hardly encroach on Isla's hospitality any further. He had an idea.

'How about I treat you to dinner

tonight at The Goose and Feather? Or somewhere else local, if there's anywhere you'd like to go?'

Isla's arm nudged his, as if they were already friends.

'Aw, that's sweet of you. Actually, I'm looking forward to an evening by the fire and watching some mindless telly. It's all I ever want after a day at the café.'

'Sure. It was just a thought.'

'I've got food in. It's yours to share.'

She smiled, the light from the streetlamp making her eyes shine. She looked cute in that yellow hat, Harry thought. He pushed the thought away.

'Well, if you're sure. Thanks, Isla. I'll get some supplies of my own in tomorrow.'

She shrugged. 'No worries. Let's just go with the flow, shall we?'

They turned the corner into Albert Street. Harry glanced at the campervan before averting his eyes. It looked lonely, standing there in the cold.

The house might have been Christmas-free — no tree, no cards or decorations, to Harry's relief — but it wasn't cat-free. Except, unlike those in The Ginger Cat, these were real.

'I hadn't realised,' he said as four cats fussed around for their supper as soon as they set foot in the door. 'I thought there was only the ginger one.'

'Nope. My aunt and uncle are cat people in every respect. They can't pass one of those cat rescue places without picking up another one.' Isla scooped up the grey cat and nuzzled its velvety ears. 'Hey, you don't mind animals, do you? You're not allergic to fur or anything?'

A laugh escaped before he could ensnare it.

'Is that funny?' Isla gave him a curious smile.

'A bit . . . no, never mind. I'm not allergic.'

'That's good then, because at least one of this lot will find its way onto your bed in the night unless you shut the door tight.' She sneezed, twice.

'You're the one who's allergic by the sound of it.'

'It gets a bit fluffy around here, that's all. My nostril linings aren't used to it.'

'No pets at home, then?'

She hadn't said where home was exactly, only that it was Nottingham. Was he indirectly pumping her for details? Perhaps. Isla was trying to avoid Christmas, the same as he was. There had to be a reason.

'Not at Mum and Dad's, no. We had a little dog when I was small, but it got old and popped its little clogs, like they do.'

'Do you live with your parents then, when you're not house-sitting?' He held up a hand. 'Sorry, none of my business. Forget I asked.'

'It's okay.' She smiled. 'I did move back home, temporarily, before I came down here. My mother's idea. I rent a flat near Nottingham town centre. I'm not sure if I'm going back there.' She turned her back on him, opening the fridge and scanning the shelves.

Had she meant she wasn't sure about going back to her flat, or to Nottingham? His curiosity roused, he wanted to know more, but she'd effectively closed off the conversation.

He wished he could tell her he understood; that he knew some subjects were off-limits because they were too painful to talk about. He sensed that about her. Behind those brown eyes he saw a world of hurt, like seeing his own soul reflected back at him.

Had they continued talking, he might have asked her what she did when she wasn't house-sitting and running a café. But then she might have asked him the same question, and he wasn't ready to share that information. Tell the world you're a vet and everyone you meet suddenly has a pet with a mystery ailment. Not that Isla with her coterie of felines would take advantage — he wouldn't mind if she did — but he'd got into the mindset of keeping quiet. Time enough after Christmas, when he'd be moving into his new rental — the ironically named Mistletoe Cottage — and joining the veterinary practice in Charnley Acre.

Several times on the journey down, he'd wondered if he should have dug his heels in and stayed put in Oxford. He'd enjoyed working at the small independent practice there, his first real job since he'd fully qualified. But in the end he'd known he had to remove himself from the place where it had all begun and ended. The place where Claudia still lived, with Steven, and the baby.

The baby he'd believed was his for four months after her conception. The baby he'd toasted in champagne whilst holding the first scan picture.

Becoming a father had never been part of the plan. One day, perhaps, but not yet. Nor had it been Claudia's plan. When she became pregnant, they'd only been together for six months; they were still getting to know one another. He'd panicked at first. He'd felt too immature to be a father; too ill-equipped. But it had happened, and he'd stepped into the future parent role. Embraced it. *Lived* it.

As it turned out, he needn't have bothered.

That sunny Sunday, the day Claudia confessed, he'd planned a relaxing outing for the two of them: a drive into the Cotswolds and lunch in a riverside pub built of honey-coloured stone. Instead, by eleven o'clock he'd found himself packing a bag and moving to a friend's place across the other side of the city. She hadn't asked him to leave, not there and then, but he'd run away because he couldn't bear to look at her for a moment longer, let alone remain in the house they shared.

And now he'd run even further. It wasn't weakness; it was a matter of self-preservation. Isla understood that — he knew it without her saying so.

They ate dinner off trays in front of the TV, with the fake coal-fire turned up high and three furry bodies slumped on the rug in front of it. The fourth — Bentley, the ginger cat — had gone prowling in the winter dark. Isla had changed her jeans for trackies with an enormous grey jumper over the top, the sleeves covering her hands. Her face gradually grew pink from the heat of the fire. They didn't talk much; there didn't seem the need to keep up a conversation just for the sake of it. At one point, Harry happened to glance at Isla just as she did the same to him. Her flash of a smile had a touch of wariness about it.

She needn't worry; he had no intention of intruding on her personal space. Isla might have secrets, but so did he. In an obscure way, it seemed to bring them together as much as sharing would.

In the middle of the quiet, black night, Harry half-woke as something heavy and soft landed against his shoulder. For one insane, dream-filled moment he thought it was Isla. But of course it wasn't. It was Bentley, seeking warmth after his nightly meanderings. He couldn't have shut the bedroom door properly.

December 22nd

Three days until Christmas

Isla sent Harry ahead to open up and make the early preparations for the day. Horace and Molly would be there; he'd be fine. Last evening had gone well. She'd hoped Harry wouldn't feel awkward about his status as unexpected guest and not know what to do with himself. Instead, he'd insisted on clearing up after she'd cooked the meal, and then he'd come and sat with her in the living room, feet up on the footstool, looking very much at home.

She'd stolen a glance at him once or twice and caught him with a pensive expression as he stared at the TV whilst not actually watching it. So far, she'd been careful not to ask questions about his circumstances, even though there were plenty of them busily burning holes in her tongue. If he wanted to talk to her, he would; there were no conditions attached to her inviting him into the house. So far, all she knew was that he'd come from Oxford, and that he had a place to stay once Christmas was over. Whether that was in Charnley Acre he hadn't said, but it didn't seem likely, given the limitations of a village this size. He'd probably ended up here by accident.

She hadn't been watching television last night any more than Harry had. Instead, she'd replayed in her head the few conversations they'd had so far to see if she could winkle out any clues. She'd found none; their chats in the café yesterday had been in general terms, light banter as they worked. There'd been no time for anything else. The same last night, over dinner. They'd talked mostly about the café, and she'd given him some background on Horace and Molly.

And then she'd woken in the small hours of the night and it had occurred to her that he might be on the run, not from actual prison — he looked too well-groomed and healthy — but from the police. Well, it wasn't so far-fetched an idea, was it? Stranger things had happened. It would be just her luck to be arrested for harbouring a criminal. Imagine explaining that one to Aunt Jo and Uncle Lloyd!

Isla wandered around the upstairs of the house in the nude — she'd not been able to do that since Harry arrived — and decided that tonight she'd try and find out more about her mystery guest. If she was in danger of being murdered in her bed, she was entitled to know.

Her mother rang on the landline just as Isla was getting out of the bath. 'You didn't ring me last night,' she said in a matter-of-fact, non-accusing voice, 'so I thought I'd see if you were all right. I'm glad I caught you.'

'Yes, sorry, Mum. I did say I'd ring, didn't I? I had a . . . ' She was going to say 'visitor' but Mum would have wanted to know who it was. Best keep quiet about that. 'I had a heavy day and went to bed early. Was it anything in particular? Is Dad okay?'

'Oh yes, your father's the same as usual. Completely disorganised — clean forgot his doctor's appointment then blamed me for not writing it on the calendar! He sends his love. No, what I wanted to tell you was . . . oh dear, I'm not sure I should say anything now.'

Isla pictured her mother's face, screwed up tight and lips pursed whenever she was in doubt. 'Mum! You can't say that then not tell me.'

Her mother's sigh breezed down the line. 'I bumped into Kate. I'd popped into your flat to check everything was all right, as I said I would, and I met her coming down the stairs afterwards. She's taken a flat in the same block, on the floor above.'

'Bloody cheek!'

'She *said*,' Mum continued, as if Isla hadn't spoken, 'she was desperately sorry for what happened and she hoped that as time went on you'd be able to forgive her. Isla, she wants to be friends again. Why else would she move close to you?'

Isla shivered and pulled the bath towel around her. Had her mother forgotten how Kate, supposedly her best friend since they were eleven, had betrayed her and hooked lead weights into her heart? Okay, it wasn't all down to her; it was Sam, too, and that was when it all fell apart.

She couldn't speak.

'Isla, forgiveness is everything. You forgave Sam, so why not Kate? It's water under the bridge.'

'Yes, I forgave Sam, you know that, otherwise I wouldn't have agreed to marry him. He made a mistake, everyone's allowed those. Kate's another story. We were a duo; we were like one person until she did what she did, and I'm not only talking about her and Sam.'

'What *are* you talking about, then? Isla?'

Isla hesitated. 'It doesn't matter. Like you said, Mum, it's all water under the bridge, and I'd like it to stay that way. It has to; I'm not that saintly. If Kate thinks we can rewind the past eighteen months and forget any of it ever happened, she's delusional. She can play her silly games and do what she bloody well likes, as long as it's nothing to do with me.'

This speech had knocked the breath out of Isla. She sat down on the top stair.

'Oh, love, I'm so stupid. I've gone and upset you now. I knew I shouldn't have told you and raked all that up again. I'm so sorry. I wish you were here and I could give you a big hug.'

Isla sensed tears, or close to. 'No, Mum, *I'm* sorry. I shouldn't have kicked off like that. You did right to tell me. Imagine how it would have been if I'd gone back to the flat and found out she was my new neighbour? No, it's fine, and *I'm* fine. You needn't worry about me. Mum? Promise you won't worry?'

'I'll do my best.' Her mother gave a little laugh. 'As long as you're all right.'

'I am, Mum. I love Charnley Acre, and the café, and I'm making new friends. It's just what I need right now.'

'Good. Well, we'll speak again soon. Before . . . '

Isla chuckled. 'Christmas. You can say it.'

Mum didn't laugh, but Isla sensed a smile. 'Yes, that. Bye, love.'

'Bye, Mum. Love you.'

Isla dressed slowly. The twin shadows of Kate and Sam had turned a shade or two darker in her mind, but she refused let them spoil her day. She moved to the window, gazing out at the silvered morning. Harry's campervan glistened as the sun melted the frost from its roof. Isla hurried the rest of her dressing and began to look forward to the busy day ahead.

* * *

In the kitchen of The Ginger Cat, Molly dreamily placed one thick slice of white crusty bread on top of another, then did it again with another round.

'What are they, then? Bread sand-wiches?'

Horace, standing next to her, took a none-too-clean hanky from his pocket and wiped his watery eyes.

It took Molly a moment to cotton on. Then she noticed the rashers of bacon resting on the hotplate. She took the top slices of bread off again and laid on the bacon.

'I don't know where your head is this morning, girl, but it ain't 'ere, that's for sure,' grumbled Horace, making off with a plate of tea cakes.

Molly pulled a face at Horace's back, making Harry, who was toasting more tea cakes, grin widely and lift his eyes in sympathy.

Molly pressed her palm down on the top layers of bread. 'Harry?'

'Yes, Molly?'

'If you'd kissed a girl, it would mean you really liked her, wouldn't it?'

Harry flinched as his fingers came into contact with the toaster grill. 'This is a hypothetical kiss, right?'

'Hypo what?'

'A made-up one.'

'Might be.'

'Well, whichever it is, yes, if I kissed a girl it would probably mean I liked her a lot. Not necessarily, though. It might just be a spur-of-the-moment thing. Or a friendly kiss.'

Molly spun round 'A *friendly* kiss? You can have those as well?'

'Not friendly, as such. Wrong word. I just meant if it was Christmas or something, then these things happen.' He looked at Molly. 'I've said the wrong thing, haven't I?'

'No, it's cool. I did ask. It wasn't Christmas, though, so it couldn't have been that.'

Her mother had said something odd this morning. It had been on Molly's mind when she'd caught her foot on a chair leg and almost sent a sausage sandwich flying into a customer's lap.

'I saw you talking to that lad across the square last night. There's nothing going on between the two of you, is there?'

Taken by surprise, Molly had felt her face going red. She'd ducked her head, pretending to look for something in her bag. 'No, course not. We were only chatting.' *Unfortunately*.

Mum had sniffed. 'Something's not right with that family.'

'What d'you mean?' Molly's head had shot up. 'Jake's really nice. There's nothing wrong with him or his family, and you shouldn't say stuff like that.'

'Oh, Moll,' Mum had said in that heavy voice she put on whenever Molly had said too much and given herself away.

'Jake's nice,' she'd repeated, for want of something else to say.

'I didn't say he wasn't. Now go on with you, off to work before you get the sack for being late.' Mum had smiled and kissed her on the cheek.

That was Mum all over, starting something and then not finishing it. Not that Molly had wanted the weirdly unsettling conversation to continue. She'd been wondering ever since why Mum had said that about Jake's family, but now she decided to stop wondering and instead think up a way to get out of going to Auntie Jean's on Christmas Eve. It was hopeless, though; she knew that.

It didn't help that her friends were texting every five minutes about Sarah's party and what they were going to wear. Molly hadn't told them she couldn't go. All the time she didn't say it, it made it less true, somehow.

Black jeggings sparkly top, she'd texted to the group as her contribution.

Which was what she would have worn to the party, had she been going. Jake had never seen her new sparkly top. Not that he'd seen much of her stuff at all, but that wasn't the point. The point was to play the game and pray for a miracle.

* * *

By eleven o'clock, half the high street had emptied itself into The Ginger Cat.

69

His eyebrows drawn together in disapproval, Horace fetched yet another pot of tea for two from the counter and deposited it with a clatter between two women with shopping bags. What people kept finding to buy was beyond him. With only three days to go, you'd have thought they would have it all in by now. It wasn't like they were getting ready for a siege, was it? The shops would be open again the day after Boxing Day. The big supermarket on the Cliffhaven Road was even open on Boxing Day itself.

'Not long now, Horace,' trilled one of the women.

'Not long till the bomb drops.' Horace slapped a sugar bowl on the table.

The women chuckled. 'Good to know you're getting in the festive spirit,' the other one said.

Truth to tell, Horace thought, shuffling back to the kitchen with some empties, he was a bit bothered about Christmas this year. Normally, he only had to consider Christmas twice, and that would be it for another year. The first time was when he bent himself double to get the artificial tree out from under the stairs — the little tree with red berries on the ends of the branches that Maureen had bought from Woolworth's in 1963 — and he only put that up out of habit.

His second consideration simply concerned his timetable for Christmas Day — what time was he expected at number eleven Albert Street for his Christmas dinner?

Maggie and her husband were usually there as well. But Maggie with her busted ankle had been carted off with her husband to stay with some old friend of hers in Brighton for the duration; he'd overheard that during a conversation in the pub. Most years, Lloyd's Auntie Doris had come over from Ringmer to make up the party. She was a pleasant enough old biddy who'd given Horace a game of rummy after the meal. But the aunt had passed on back in the spring, which left Horace as the only guest.

Still, he had no reason to suppose his

regular invitation wouldn't stand this year. The girl, Isla, was Jo's niece — proper family, not any old sausage they'd hired to fill in. She'd been installed to look after the café, the house and the four moth-eaten moggies that went with it. Surely she was under instructions to take on the Christmas dinner arrangements as well?

The trouble was, no matter what Horace thought should happen, nothing had been said. And, as had just been pointed out to him, the day itself was fast approaching. He'd have to say something, that was plain. Maybe drop it into the conversation in passing, like, and see what came of it. He should do it today. There was no time to waste if he wasn't going to dine on overcooked rabbit stew on Christmas Day.

He'd been so engrossed in chewing over his problem that Horace hadn't noticed Olive Cowstick come in and squeeze her bulk into the corner table until it was too late to hide himself. Her plump cheeks were bright pink from the cold, reminding Horace of the round raspberry-iced buns in the cabinet. She was already yoo-hooing at him across the café, which meant that the others would give her a wide berth — God knew she needed one — and leave him to do the honours.

'Enjoyed your dinner last night, did you?' Olive leaned conspiratorially towards Horace as he scribbled down her order of tea and double poached eggs on toast.

Horace pulled himself upright, pressing his shoulders back. 'Can't say I didn't. It was a fair old spread you put on there.'

Olive went to pat Horace's hand. He whipped it away fast before she could make contact.

'That's it, then. We should stick together, us widowed ones.' She winked — at least Horace interpreted the lift of one cheek and twist of her mouth as a wink, even though her actual eye didn't move.

'I'll fetch your tea,' he said.

For some reason, the counter suddenly seemed very far away, and his feet didn't seem to want to move. It was as if Olive had him on a length of elastic.

No sooner was he back with the pot of tea, having handed the order for the eggs to Isla, than she was off again.

'Like I said last night, if you get behind and want me to give your house a bottoming, you've only got to shout. I can always fit you in.'

I bet you can, Horace thought. Nothing better to do than come round interfering, more like.

'I do all right,' he said. 'Ta for the offer, though.' A little thank-you wouldn't do any harm. He couldn't be too ungentlemanly, especially after the gammon dinner.

'Any time, Horace.' The wink again, unless she had a bit of grit in her eye and was trying to work it out. 'And while I'm about it, how would you like to come round to mine on Christmas Day, for your dinner?'

Horace reeled back. He felt his neck stiffen.

'Ah, I knew you'd be pleased!' Olive said triumphantly. 'I love a good old-fashioned turkey dinner, me. Plenty of roast spuds and all the trimmings. Not worth doing just for one. There's Christmas pud for after. I made it myself, back in August. They're at their best when they're well matured.' She chuckled. 'Like us, eh, Horace?'

Horace looked desperately towards the counter, just as Isla placed the plate of poached eggs on top and gave him the nod. He stomped off, grateful for the ten-second breather.

'Truth is, Olive,' he said, returning with her lunch, 'I'm already committed, like. I always have me Christmas dinner along at Albert Street.' He gave a backwards nod of his head towards Isla.

Olive's eyebrows shot up in surprise. 'Oh, what's that, then? Staff perks?'

'No, no. Nought to do with that. Same every year.'

'But they're away, our Jo, and her hubby.'

Horace shrugged, feigning a casual

confidence he didn't feel. 'Makes no odds. Albert Street is where I'll be on the day, same as always.'

He could almost see the cogs of Olive's brain whirring. As well they might. Well, it was done now. He'd have to tackle Isla, and sharpish.

★ ★ ★

Isla arrived back at Albert Street before Harry. They'd cleared up the café together, then Harry had gone to the mini-supermarket to pick up a few items he needed while Isla carried on home. By the time Harry came in, she'd showered and changed, and a fish pie was in the oven.

'You don't need to cook for me,' he said. 'I'm happy to take my turn, or we can just do our own thing. I'll take second dibs at the cooker.'

She smiled. 'Don't be daft. It makes sense to share.'

'In that case — ' He delved into the carrier bag he'd brought in. '— here's my contribution to tonight.' He held up a bottle of red wine. 'I got white as well, in case you prefer that?'

'The thing is,' Isla said, feeling the familiar flood of heat to her face. 'I don't drink.'

She watched Harry struggle to hide his surprise, which was how most people reacted.

'Okay. Mind if I stick the white one in the fridge?'

'Of course. Put the red in the bottom of the larder, or stand it anywhere. I'll put my elderflower fizz in a wine glass to keep you company.'

Harry looked doubtful. 'I don't have to. I can take both across to the van.'

'No, I'm fine around other people drinking. It's just not for me. Not anymore.' She let a beat of silence fall. 'Harry, I've got a bit of a problem.'

'With alcohol?'

She laughed. 'No, I didn't mean that.'

Harry's *faux pas* wasn't as funny as she made out. Not funny at all. But he wasn't to know that.

'Sorry, Isla. I seem to have put my foot in it.'

She shrugged. 'It's fine. Shall we start that last bit again?'

'Please.'

'Right, well, technically, *we* have a problem. It's Horace.'

'Don't tell me he's gone lame or something?'

'Lame?' Isla giggled, thinking of horses, or dogs. 'No, listen. Horace is expecting to have Christmas dinner here, with us.'

'But we weren't . . . '

'Exactly. And even if we were, Aunt Jo and Uncle Lloyd didn't say anything about Horace coming, which apparently he has for the last twenty years on the trot. Well, not *twenty*, but you get my drift.'

'Do you think he's telling the truth, or is he taking advantage of your relatives being away?'

'The absolute truth, I could tell. Horace isn't that devious.'

Harry dropped onto a chair. 'What did you say?'

'I said I might have to do some reorganising and I'd let him know for definite tomorrow.' She sighed, remembering Horace's downturned mouth, his lugubrious expression. He hadn't asked her outright — even Horace was too circumspect for that — but he had expressed it in such a way that it came out as a veiled ultimatum. He'd cornered Isla while she was in the small staff area next to the kitchen, using her laptop to place orders with the suppliers for the new year.

'Olive — that's her who was in earlier, had the poached eggs,' Horace had said, half whispering as if he was afraid of being overheard, 'she's asked me round to hers for me Christmas dinner. Only I told her, I told her straight out, like, I'd made my promise to you to have it at Albert Street, because I said to her, Olive, I said, just because Jo and Lloyd aren't here doesn't mean things won't stay the same this year, and I ain't in the habit of letting folks down. I always bring a bottle of sherry and a box of after-dinner mints. Just so's you know.'

This speech, with no pause for breath, had made Horace's chest wheeze a tune and the cords on his scrawny neck stand out quite alarmingly.

Isla had swallowed hard. 'I see,' she'd said. 'So it's usually Christmas dinner at Albert Street, turkey, stuffing and the full works, in the middle of the day, presumably?'

'Gawd, yes,' Horace had stuttered, as if any other form of catering on Christmas Day would result in a feudal uprising. Which it possibly might, knowing Charnley Acre.

'Does anyone else come to this Christmassy feast?' she'd asked, thinking she might as well get this over and done with in one shot.

'There's Maggie, who works here, and her husband.'

'Is there?' Isla had felt weak.

Horace held up a gnarled finger. 'They've gone to Brighton, having it with some friend of hers.'

'Not Maggie and her husband, then. Is that it?'

'Lloyd's Auntie Doris. I beat her at rummy after dinner last year. And the year before that.'

'I didn't know my uncle had an Auntie Doris.'

'He don't now. She's dead.'

'So it's just you, then?' Isla had felt a thin thread of hope winding itself through her.

'Yes. Well, I'll sees you about it tomorrow, then.' Horace had nodded firmly, making sure they'd got it straight before he went home.

'What do I do?' Isla held out her hands, palms up, and appealed to Harry to get her — them — out of this.

'I'm thinking,' Harry said, getting up and pouring himself a glass of red wine. He came back to the table. 'I know. You could tell him that with your aunt and uncle being away, things will be different this year. Keep it vague.'

'I could, but then he might ask what I am doing for Christmas and it wouldn't feel right to tell him I'm not doing anything, even if it is true. Horace is an old man, he's been widowed a number of years, he's a loyal employee. I can see why Lloyd and Jo started inviting him. It's a pity they didn't think to mention that tiny detail before they left. There was so much else to tell me they must have forgotten.'

'He's got Olive now, by the sound of it,' Harry said.

'Oh, he's been trying to escape her clutches for ages, from what Molly told me.' Isla laughed. 'She can be quite fearsome.'

'Her heart must be in the right place if she's invited him for Christmas. And I heard she gave him dinner last night at Malt Cottage.'

'*Did* she? Good old Olive. She must be making progress.'

'So . . . ' Harry gave her a pointed look.

'So, we leave Horace's Christmas blow-out in the capable hands of Olive Cowstick. Is that what you're saying?'

'Maybe.'

Isla held up a finger. 'Ah, you see? You're weakening already.'

Harry sipped some wine. 'I get the impression there's more to Horace under that dour exterior than meets the eye. He told me he used to work at the Savoy in London, back in the day.'

'Yes, the Savoy café in the East End. It's a greasy spoon, or it was. I fell for that one, too, until Maggie tipped me off.'

Harry laughed. 'Good old Horace.'

'So do I relent and invite the old devil for his Christmas dinner? Or rather, do *we* invite him? You're part of this, too. Unless you want to spend the day cooped up in a freezing campervan with a tin of baked beans.'

As she spooned fish pie onto plates, Isla thought how fast things had turned around. Two days ago, she'd been alone in the house, apart from the cats, and happy to be so, until she'd gone all neighbourhood-watch and decided to investigate the campervan. And now here was her unexpected guest — a handsome one at that — making himself at home at her kitchen table. On top of that, her carefully orchestrated non-Christmas looked like becoming, well, Christmas.

'If we don't let him come here, what's the likelihood of him turning down Olive's invitation and being on his own for Christmas?' Harry said.

Isla sighed. 'No idea. But it's Christmas, the time of goodwill, and all that. Oh God, I've talked myself into it, haven't I?'

Harry grinned. 'Yep. Looks like we've got shopping to do.'

'Let's not think about that tonight,' Isla said. 'Perhaps Horace will have changed his mind by the morning and decided Olive's the better option.'

'You don't really think that.'

'No, I don't. Perhaps it won't be so bad. Horace will be here, what, two hours, three at most? And then you and I can carry on with forgetting all about Christmas.'

'Won't he expect decorations — a tree, at least?'

Isla held up a hand. 'Oh no, I'm not going that far. He won't notice if we feed him well.'

Sixpence, the grey cat, padded into the kitchen and jumped onto Harry's lap, wedging herself between him and the table. Harry rubbed the cat's ears absently as he gazed unseeingly towards the black square of the window. Isla wondered what he was thinking about. She remembered her decision to find out more about her guest, but with all the talk about Horace, there'd been no lead-in to the right sort of conversation. She'd have to remain curious, for now.

Taking her cue from Harry, Isla let silence prevail. She thought back to this morning's conversation with her mother. The full-on day at the café and her own determination to remain cheerful had successfully kept thoughts of Kate at bay. Now, the barriers came down and the memories flooded in. She saw herself and Kate in some bar or other, flirting outrageously with the barman, and joshing with any blokes who happened to be around. Drunk or not, they'd never gone further than flirting and joking about — they weren't that wild, or stupid. But they'd made spectacles of themselves in other ways, dancing on tables, fooling about in the street. And all too frequently, throwing up in the gutter — that was Isla, never Kate.

They were young; Nottingham was a party town, and they were ready to party.

It had taken Isla a long time to realise that Kate never drunk as much as she did. But Kate possessed all the self-confidence that Isla lacked, and she had control. Isla didn't. Not then. It was a crazy time, a dangerous time. A time of no shame.

It was always Kate who got Isla home after these nights of madness, via the house Kate shared, if Isla was in too much of a state to go straight home to her parents' house where she lived at the time. That way, her parents were never aware of the extent of Isla's drinking, and she'd been grateful to Kate for allowing that protection.

But, in the end, Kate had turned out to be a false friend. Singlehandedly, she'd shattered Isla's faith in just about everyone, including herself. And, of course, in Sam.

★   ★   ★

Isla had gone upstairs after they'd eaten. Harry loaded the dishwasher then sat in the living room, reading the paper he'd bought. A while later, when she hadn't reappeared, he took himself off to the campervan. The weather had turned unseasonably mild during the day and the little heater in the van was enough to keep it cosy enough to sit in for a while. Isla seemed very relaxed about him being in the house. Consequently, he felt comfortable being there, but it seemed only fair to give her some space. They were together all day, after all.

Closing the curtains against the murky

night, he took out the paperwork pertaining to his new job and had another read through. His contract was for one year initially, covering a vet on maternity leave which, in his current situation of having no long-term plan, suited him fine. As for the village itself, from his two days working at The Ginger Cat, he knew he could do a lot worse than Charnley Acre. The locals he'd met in the shops and the pub, as well as the café, were friendly and down to earth. It might be a typical village in that the ins and outs of people's lives were fair game for a spot of gossip, but from what he'd heard so far, it was harmless enough.

Next, having put the paperwork back in his case, he rang his mother and told her about his job in The Ginger Cat. She met this news with her usual bright enthusiasm, admitting she'd been worrying about him being lonely and how pleased she was that he had people around him during the day. She didn't ask where he was staying, probably imagining he'd already moved into

Mistletoe Cottage — either that or he was sitting it out in the van. Harry didn't enlighten her. Neither did he ask her what she was doing for Christmas, it being a delicate subject.

She told him anyway. 'It's just the two of us we've booked in at Hartshaw Manor. They do a wonderful Christmas Day menu and it'll make a nice change not to have to peel a hundred sprouts!'

Her laughter reached Harry's ears, sharp and shiny, like polished steel. He flinched at the unnatural sound. She was overcompensating in her attempt to lessen his guilt at not being home for Christmas. And, perhaps, to lessen his heartache. If she could have taken his pain upon herself and freed him of it, he knew she wouldn't hesitate.

His father had died when Harry was a teenager. Mum had remarried, to a kind, intelligent man who was much like his father in many ways. Harry imagined the pair of them, arm in arm, strolling to the riverside restaurant to have their Christmas dinner among strangers — not at all the kind of day his mother must have envisaged. She'd played down her own loss of Claudia, whom she'd got on with rather well, and the granddaughter-who-wasn't, for Harry's sake, but at this time of year she must be feeling it keenly.

'Sounds like a plan,' he said. 'You have a good time, and I'll ring again soon.'

The call ended, and Harry stretched out on the banquette seat, hands behind his head, and thought about Claudia.

They'd met in a smart bistro, nothing like the pubs and bars with a student vibe that he and his mates usually favoured, but it had been somebody's birthday. Claudia had been among a group of female friends also celebrating a birthday. The two groups had melded together as the evening went on. He and Claudia had got chatting, and he couldn't believe his luck when she agreed to swap mobile numbers.

She'd dropped her current boyfriend like a hot stone to go out with him; flattering at the time, but later — much later — he'd felt her treatment of her ex signalled something about her. She'd been working for a public relations company at the time, doing what precisely he'd never really known. She didn't talk much about the work itself, only about the people she came into contact with, as if the social side of the job was all that mattered.

Harry's mates had envied him dating Claudia. Tall and slender, creamy-skinned and blue-eyed, her hair a pale gold curtain of silk down her back, she drew admiring looks. Harry's mother called her an English rose.

But roses had thorns.

Harry's mind drifted to Isla. As far as looks went, she was the opposite of Claudia. She was medium height with a figure that was compact rather than willowy; her skin was the sort that tanned easily in summer. The bottom two inches of her dark brown hair, which fell to just below chin level, were dyed purple.

Isla presented a happy, carefree persona to the world, bustling around the café with a big smile on her face, but Harry knew a broken heart when he saw one. He wished he could help, but if she wouldn't talk to him, there was nothing he could do.

Turning his head sideways, he looked between the gap in the flimsy curtains of the van towards number eleven. The light had gone out in the living room, and a dim light showed in the window above; Isla's bedroom. It was still early, only nine o'clock. Had she gone to bed already? He couldn't help feeling a little disappointed. It had been a long day, though, and looked like being the same tomorrow.

Harry sat up, thinking he might walk up to The Goose and Feather for a pint, when he heard voices coming from the pavement side of the van. He peered through the curtains, feeling like a voyeur. Two people had entered the park and were crossing the dark swath of grass. The area around the kiddies' playground was lit by a streetlamp, and as they moved into the pool of light, he saw that one of them was Molly. The other was a male he didn't recognise. He seemed to be walking fast, Molly trotting along behind. The boy, whoever he was, suddenly stopped and turned round, and Molly reeled back. The voices had been faint, but now the boy's voice rose, and Molly swung round on her heel and ran across the grass, back to the park entrance, and set off along Albert Street, towards the high street.

Harry held on for a few minutes, allowing her to get a head start. If she'd had a tiff with her boyfriend, she was best left alone. She wouldn't want the embarrassment of bumping into him while she was upset. Remembering the question she'd asked him about kissing, he hoped she was okay. She was a likeable girl, if a bit of a Dolly-Daydream at times.

There was no sign of Molly as Harry made his way to The Goose. Being so close to Christmas, the place was packed. Drawn into the general banter and willingly inveigled into a game of darts, it was almost closing time before he wandered contentedly back to Albert Street.

Surprisingly, the downstairs lights were back on. Isla was in the kitchen with all four cats. Treacle and Whisky were noisily crunching biscuits at the feeding bowls, Sixpence sat on the draining board, and Isla had Bentley, the ginger cat, on the kitchen table, cupping his broad face with both hands and peering closely at him.

She cast a worried glance at Harry as he entered. 'Bentley's not right. He's dribbling a lot. He's not happy at all, and he's not eating.'

Harry's instinct sent him close up to the table to get a better look. 'When did he last eat?'

'What? Oh, I don't know exactly. Last night, maybe. I didn't see him go up to the bowls at breakfast, although he might have, I didn't stop to watch. He's definitely not interested in supper. I opened him a special tin of tuna, too.'

Bentley's head drooped as Isla stroked his ears.

'If he's not better by the morning, I'll get him to the vet's and hope they can fit him in. They'll have to see him if it's an emergency, won't they?' She looked at Harry. 'It's quite a responsibility when it's somebody else's pet, especially when you know naff all about them.'

'Dribbling, you say?'

'Yes, look, it's all down his chin. Perhaps he's got toothache. Wouldn't it be awful if he was in pain?'

'May I look?'

Isla turned surprised eyes on Harry. 'If you like, but there's nothing to see apart from the dribble. He won't let me look in his mouth.'

'Hold him upright for me, nice and firm. Don't let him go.'

Isla frowned, but did as she was asked. While Isla held the cat steady, Harry took hold of his jaw, prised it open and stooped down to peer inside. The over-head light helped.

'Right. Hold him there and I'll be back in a tick.'

'Harry? Where are you going?' he heard as he opened the front door.

Moments later, he returned with his

case. Isla was still holding on to Bentley, with difficulty as the cat was starting to struggle.

'Just another minute, if you can.' Opening the case and unfolding the pack of instruments, he selected a pair of fine tweezers and opened the cat's mouth again.

'Ah ha. Got it!' He held up a long, curved bone. 'This the culprit. He'd got it wedged clean across the roof of his mouth and caught between his teeth.' He dropped the thin white bone onto the table. 'Looks like a chicken bone. Probably got it out of somebody's rubbish.'

Bentley jumped down off the table and vanished ungratefully through the cat flap.

'That's amazing! How did you know what to do? Oh . . . ' Isla looked at Harry, then at the unfolded case with its range of instruments. She laughed. 'You're a vet! Bloody hell, Harry, why didn't you say?'

He shrugged. 'It didn't come up.'

'I suppose I've only got myself to blame. I've told you zilch about me.'

She tucked a stray strand of hair behind one ear. It immediately fell forward again. It was only then that Harry noticed she was wearing pyjamas; silky turquoise-coloured ones, with wide-legged trousers which obscured her bare feet, revealing only the tips of her toes. The top was a kind of strappy vest which left little to the imagination. He averted his eyes, but not before he'd spotted the tiny flower tattooed on her left shoulder.

'You didn't have to tell me anything. I've not been exactly forthcoming myself.'

'It's not always that easy, is it?'

'Not always, no. As it happens, I'm joining the practice in the high street after Christmas, and I'll be moving into a little place called Mistletoe Cottage when the current tenant moves out.'

'You're staying here, in Charnley Acre?' Isla's brown eyes were wide. 'And there was me, having visions of you taking off after Christmas in the campervan and stopping off wherever the fancy took you. It seemed kind of romantic.'

'Ha, well, sorry to disappoint, but getting down here from Oxford in that thing was quite enough. I borrowed the van from a mate and left my car at his. It was all a bit last-minute. I suddenly knew I couldn't wait for the job to start and the cottage to be ready. I had to get away.'

'From . . . ?'

Isla's eyes were on his. She was genuinely concerned as well as interested.

'From the woman I'd planned to spend the rest of my life with. The woman who got pregnant by somebody else and pretended the baby was mine until it didn't suit her to keep up the lie any longer.'

'Oh Harry, that's awful. How could you be sure the baby wasn't yours?' Isla paused. 'Sorry, I take that back. I shouldn't have asked.'

'It's okay. When she confessed, I sat down and worked out the dates for myself, and I realised that at the time the baby would have been conceived I was recovering from an appendectomy. I was as sore as hell. There was no way I could have . . . not for weeks. Anyway, Claudia's with Steven now. The little girl was born a few months ago.'

'They still live in Oxford?'

'Yep. Playing happy families.'

'No wonder you wanted to get away.'

'There were too many reminders everywhere I looked. Who needs those? I decided to give myself a fighting chance and head for the hills — literally, Sussex being full of the damn things.'

A brief smile touched Isla's lips. She let a beat of silence fall before she said, 'I'm having tea. Do you want some?'

'Please. Here, let me.'

Harry filled the kettle. He wondered if, over the tea, Isla would tell him her own story, but she didn't.

'Looks like we've both been let down, big time,' was all she said before she picked up her mug of tea and went off upstairs.

December 23rd

Two days until Christmas

Isla and Harry had made a shopping list first thing, and Harry had set off in the campervan for the supermarket on the Cliffhaven Road. Isla had given him unnecessarily detailed instructions about checking the use-by dates on the turkeys, and if they didn't have the right size fresh ones, to go for frozen but only if he really had to. He'd accepted all this with good humour, and told her not to worry.

That was easier said than done. It felt like a huge responsibility, cooking Christmas dinner for somebody who was not family, and who clearly had high expectations of culinary perfection — Horace, that was, not Harry.

Isla had woken several times in the night with Harry's revelation on her mind. What a bitch Claudia must be! And how devastating for Harry, believing he was about to become a father when all the time she was hiding that secret. How could anybody be that cruel?

She'd almost told Harry about Sam and Kate and the non-wedding but it had been late, they were both tired, and it wouldn't have felt right to counter Harry's story with her own. Whether she would tell him eventually remained to be seen. Christmas would be over in a flash, and Harry would move into Mistletoe Cottage and take up his post at the vets' surgery. Would there still be a chance to talk to him then?

He would be busy making his new life, making new friends. And she would carry on as she was, trying not to think about what might have been, and waiting on Aunt Jo and Uncle Lloyd's return at the end of January. After that . . . well, she'd not thought that far ahead, even if it was only a matter of weeks away.

That was the trouble with running away. Sooner or later, you had to decide whether to go back, or keep running.

Horace was already at the café by the time Isla arrived, hovering just inside the door with an anxious look on his face.

'Good. You're 'ere. Only, there's no fruit scones left and no plain ones either.'

'Yes there are, there are tons in the freezer.' Frowning, Isla went through to the kitchen, Horace close behind. She pulled out the plastic boxes containing the scones. 'Cheese. Cheese. More cheese.' She turned to Horace. 'How the hell did that happen?'

'Search me,' Horace said. 'We could say they're off the menu.'

'Looks like we'll have to. There's only today and tomorrow to go, and tomorrow we'll shut after lunch. Nobody will expect us to be open on Christmas Eve afternoon.'

'We *could* say. Except we can't.'

'Can't we?' Isla was struggling to follow.

'No. We got the receptionists, the nurses and the foot lady from the medical centre in at two for cream teas. Or rather, you have — I'll be gone 'ome by then. One of 'em popped in yesterday to make sure it was all right, like.'

'And you said it was.'

'Course! They come every year for their Christmas treat. Can't let 'em down.'

Isla took off her coat and hat and went to hang them up, thinking hard while she did so.

'Okay,' she said, spinning round and cannoning into Horace, who seemed to be following her every move. 'It's not a problem. I can make a batch of scones by two o'clock. The recipe will be in the folder.'

She'd only made scones once before, at school. They'd turned out hard enough to crack windows, as a girl in her class had gone right ahead and proved.

Horace tilted his head doubtfully. 'Will they be as good as Maggie's? Only, if they ain't . . . ' He pursed his lips and drew in air.

'Well, I don't what else I'm meant to

do.' Isla felt the strings of stress pulling through her shoulders. 'Either I have a go or we sell the medical staff something we *have* got.'

'Or . . . ' Horace raised a veiny finger. 'I could get us a bit of help.'

'Could you? How?'

Horace tapped the side of his nose. 'Leave it with me. Oh, and while we're 'ere, did you have the chance to do your reorganising, like you said yesterday?'

Reorganising? Isla saw Horace's expression soften, his lips curling into a semblance of a smile, and remembered.

She smiled in return. 'Yes, I did, Horace, and you'll be very welcome to come to number eleven Albert Street for your Christmas dinner. Kick-off at one o'clock.'

Horace's face turned even pinker than usual, and his rheumy eyes lit up.

'That's mighty good of you,' he said. 'Now, you leave them scones to me.'

Slightly bemused, Isla went behind the counter and began on the coffee orders Horace had taken for two early arrivals.

She smiled to herself. If Horace thought he'd blackmailed his way into securing his Christmas dinner invitation, he'd wasted his time, since she'd been going to invite him anyway.

'Just poppin' out,' he said. He went to the door, then turned round. 'One other thing.'

'Yes, Horace?'

'Our Molly's out the back sobbin' her heart out. Cheery-bye!' The café door clicked shut, with Horace on the other side of it.

The door immediately opened again and three women entered and chose a table. They all had bulging carrier bags from the butcher's.

Isla delivered the coffees to the earlier customers, told the new arrivals she'd be back in a minute, then went in search of Molly. She hadn't even realised the girl had arrived.

Molly was standing against the wall beside the bins out in the yard. Her eyes were red-rimmed, and rivulets of black mascara trickled down her cheeks.

'Molly? Whatever's the matter? You're shivering. Come inside. Now.'

Isla's voice came out with unintentional sharpness. But really, this was all she needed this morning. Molly lifted herself away from the wall and obediently followed Isla into the kitchen.

'Now, what's this all about?' Isla said, thinking it had better be quick as there was nobody out in the café at all, now Horace had hiked off.

Molly let out a strangled sob, then reined it in with a heavy sniff. 'I'm sorry. I'll be okay in a minute, honest.'

'Molly, has something happened?' Isla's mind whirred around the possibilities which, Molly being a teenager, were many and varied.

'I did something really stupid last night.'

Isla's heart dipped. Did she mean . . . ? 'To do with a boy?' Isla ventured, not wanting to know the answer.

Molly nodded, her big blue eyes fixed on the floor.

The café door clicked again.

'Look, I can't talk now. There's nobody left serving. Sit down, have a cup of tea, and I'll come back as soon as I can, okay?'

Molly seemed to gather herself. 'It's not what it sounded like. I'm sorry to be a nuisance. I'll be out in a minute.'

'Well, if you're sure,' Isla said kindly. 'Wash your face first, though.' She smiled at Molly and dashed back to the café.

As she took the orders from three women, Horace came past the window. He wasn't alone. Puffing along behind him was Olive Cowstick. Horace barged into the café first, leaving Olive to catch hold of the swinging door.

'We're sorted,' Horace said, following Isla to the counter. 'Scone-wise, that is.' He nodded over his shoulder towards Olive.

Isla looked from one to the other of them, confused.

'Scones, plain and fruit,' Olive said, beaming widely, her face almost as red as her coat. 'Coupla dozen of each do you?'

'Yes, but . . . '

'Lead on,' Olive said unnecessarily, since she was already behind the counter and entering the kitchen. 'Show me where everything is and I'll make a start.' She held up two bulging carrier bags. 'Just in case you're out of ingredients, I brought me own.'

She dumped the bags on the work surface. Among the contents, Isla saw bags of flour, sugar, and blocks of butter. At least something was going right this morning.

'Oh, Olive, would you? That would be marvellous. Thank you.'

'No worries, duck. Horace here has a silver tongue. Knows how to get round a girl.' She gave a sort of wink.

Isla suppressed a giggle. She cleared a space for her saviour to work in, and switched the big oven on.

'There should enough flour and stuff, but if you have to use any of your own, I'll reimburse you. As well as paying you for your time, of course.'

'I don't want paying, lovely. It'll be

my pleasure.' Olive aimed her beam at Horace, who made a rapid retreat to the café.

Isla was about to follow him when she remembered Molly, and doubled back. No new customers had arrived; Horace could manage on his own for a while.

Molly was at the sink, gulping back water from a glass.

'She all right?' Olive directed a floury thumb towards Molly.

Isla made a *no idea* face at Olive. Molly banged the glass down and turned round. Her face was clean and shiny; she looked almost back to normal.

'I'm sorry I made such a fuss. Can I go and put my make-up back on? Then I'll get started.'

'Yes, of course. But if you want to talk, grab me later, okay?'

'Okay.'

Isla wished Harry was back — she could do with seeing his friendly face — but he'd be ages yet. The shopping list had covered two sides of the paper.

The supermarket would be thronging, and he had to drive back to Albert Street and drop off the shopping.

The Ginger Cat filled up. Coffees and breakfasts turned to elevenses and early lunches. Chat and laughter rose from the tables in the excitement about Christmas. Isla tried to shut her ears to it, but it wasn't easy to ignore the festive atmosphere and look cheerful at the same time. Horace traipsed between tables and counter wearing a fixed, toothy grin, no doubt with extra Christmas tips in mind. Behind the counter, Molly dropped two saucers — both smashed — then went into a trance as she squirted cream on top of a hot chocolate and forgot to take her finger off the button, covering the side of the mug, the saucer and half the counter in froth.

Raising her eyes, Isla retreated to the relative peace of the kitchen in time to see a wodge of scone dough leave Olive's large red hands and land on the pastry board in a cloud of flour.

'Just got to cut these out, then that's

the first lot ready for the oven.'

'You're an absolute wonder,' Isla said. 'Please take a break, Olive. I'll get you a coffee, or tea, whatever you want. And choose a cake from the cabinet.'

'Ooh yes, I could go a nice cup of tea. Whenever you're ready, like.'

★　★　★

As the delicious aroma of baking filled the air, Isla felt close to gaining control. Harry still hadn't returned, but Horace and Molly, who seemed to have got her act together, were managing well between them.

'Thank you for bringing Olive,' Isla said as Horace collected three gingerbread people from the cabinet for the children who'd come in with their parents. 'You saved the day there. The scones are marvellous. I tried one.'

'You're welcome,' Horace said, avoiding Isla's eye.

'Is Olive a particular friend of yours, then?'

Horace grimaced. 'She'd like to be, let's put it that way.'

'Well, what's wrong with that? She's on her own, too, isn't she? You can't blame her for seeking a bit of company.'

'She still out there?' Horace nodded towards the kitchen.

'Yes, she insisted on clearing up after her scone-making, though I told her I'd do it. Now she's slicing the scones in half and whipping the cream for the cream teas. It's very kind of her to help out, isn't it?'

'Yes, well . . . ' Horace said. 'I shall want me ciggie break in a minute.'

Isla looked for the connection. It came to her — Horace didn't want to go past Olive to reach the yard.

'Oh, I'm sure you'll be safe enough.' Isla winked.

Horace looked bashful. 'I'm not so sure about that.' He held up the plate of gingerbread people. ''Ere, look at this lot.'

Isla looked. 'The icing's gone a bit wonky. Never mind, they'll taste the same and the kids won't notice.'

'Their mums and dads might. Have another look.'

Isla looked, then broke into giggles. The gingerbread people were bought in but iced on the premises. The female ones always had icing frills round their shoulders and another frill lower down, suggesting a skirt; the male versions had V-shaped collars and straight lines for trousers. Both were supposed to have two circles down the front to denote buttons. The frills and lines hadn't been too badly executed, but the buttons had fallen way short of their target. Each biscuit had two lopsided circles side by side, with stray dots of icing in the middle.

'They've all got titties, see?' Horace whispered. 'Even the blokes.'

'So they have. Who iced them?'

'Who d'you think?' Horace nodded towards Molly. 'She done 'em first thing, before she went into a decline.'

Isla was still laughing. 'Just serve them, Horace. It's Christmas. When you've fin-ished that table, come with me through to the back, then you can have your ciggie.'

Placated, Horace trudged off while Isla served more coffees. Then, checking that Molly was coping, she went through to the kitchen, Horace close behind her as if he was glued on.

'Ah, here he is!' cried Olive. 'I was wondering where you'd got to.'

'I've been out there working. Where did you think I'd got to?' Horace glowered at Olive but made no move to go out for his ciggie.

'I can't thank you enough, Olive,' Isla said. 'Let me sort out some money for you.' She held up a hand. 'I know what you said, but fair's fair.' She had a thought. 'Olive, would you like to come to Albert Street for your Christmas dinner? Horace is coming, aren't you, Horace?'

'Well, now, that would be splendid, if you're sure. I'd be on me own otherwise. Very kind.'

'Lord, give me strength,' Horace muttered, and headed for the back door.

Harry's mobile rang as he was unloading carrier bags in the kitchen of number eleven and wondering how a simple roast dinner could possibly need so many ingredients.

'Are you okay? Are you home yet?' Isla sounded rather out of breath.

'Just got in. I'm fine, although the supermarket was a baptism of fire. Clau . . . we used to shop online.'

'What size turkey did you get?'

'Size? As in weight?' Harry said, deliberately prevaricating.

'No, I mean how many will it feed? Only, we've got an extra guest. I invited Olive Cowstick — I'll tell you about that later.'

Harry eyed the mountainous shrink-wrapped bird on the table. It looked even more enormous now than it had in the chiller cabinet. He'd wavered between turkeys that fed four to six people, which looked a bit on the mean side, and those that fed ten to twelve — there'd been none left in between — and decided to play safe. There were always the cats.

'Yep, there'll be plenty for Olive.'

And most of Sussex.

'Good. Well done. See you soon.' She was gone.

Harry eyed the turkey again, then opened the oven door and looked inside. If they moved the shelves about it might just fit, although from his best guess, it would scrape the sides. The roast potatoes could go in the small second oven, if it got hot enough.

Harry shut the oven door. It was no use worrying now. He and Isla would no doubt go into conference tonight. Meanwhile, the damn thing had to be refrigerated. It took a while to take everything out of the fridge, shift the shelves about, wedge the turkey in and then fit everything else around it.

A beautiful vision floated across his mind of an ordinary December the 25th: a day like any other. A walk, a film on DVD, shepherd's pie for dinner, and no necessity to be jolly if he didn't feel like it. The vision taunted him before gently floating out of sight. It seemed to be waving goodbye rather smugly.

Harry gave himself a mental shake. Isla seemed to be coping pretty well with having her non-Christmas hijacked. He should take a tip from her and just get on with it.

Olive Cowstick, though? Harry was chuckling to himself as he set off for The Ginger Cat. Actually, that was a shrewd move on Isla's part. He'd been wondering, in a fairly non-interested kind of way, whether Christmas dinner with just the three of them would be a silent, awkward affair. No danger of that now.

Isla cornered Harry as soon as he entered the café and went behind the counter. He heard a rapid account of Olive's scone-making activities before Isla moved on to the subject of Molly.

'She says she's fine now, but look at her.'

Harry looked. Molly's normally cheerful smile had a forced look about it, and the china on her tray rattled even more perilously than usual as she wove a distracted path between the tables. He remembered last night — Molly and the boy in the park; Molly running off as if she was upset.

'It'll be boy trouble. I wouldn't worry.' Harry glanced around the packed café. 'Doesn't look like we've got time to worry anyway. Why are those tables pushed together?'

'Medical centre staff. Cream teas at two. Oh God, I forgot to do the jam pots, and we're out of clean teaspoons!'

Isla dashed off to the kitchen, leaving Harry to interpret Molly's orders with their many crossings-out.

$$\star \quad \star \quad \star$$

Molly had lain awake for most of the night in a sweat of misery. If Jake ever spoke to her again it would be a miracle. Which was a good thing, because if he ever did speak to her again, she would totally die of embarrassment on the spot.

She'd been walking home from Kathryn's house last night, her other friends having gone in a different direction, when she'd spotted Jake walking ahead. She'd broken into a trot to catch up with him, imagining them walking back to Honeypot Square together. And then, if her lucky star had happened to be shining, he might have asked her out on a date. Or, if not exactly that, he might have wanted to know if she was going to Sarah's Christmas Eve party, and look disappointed when she said she wasn't.

He must have heard footsteps behind him but he hadn't turned round, so she'd called his name, just once. He must have heard that, too. But he'd walked right on, quickening his pace.

She should have taken the hint, hung back and let him reach the square before she did. Oh, why hadn't she done that? Instead, she'd walked faster, trailing him as he'd turned into Albert Street, until eventually she'd drawn level with him on the opposite side of the road. It could have been the vodka somebody had sneaked into Kathryn's house — she could easily blame it on that, although she'd only had a drop. Whatever, she'd called out again, and that time he'd had to glance across. She'd waved before prancing over the road to land by his side.

'Watcha, Molly.' He'd hardly looked at her.

'Are you walking home?' she'd asked. Dumb question.

'Yup.'

'I'll walk with you then, shall I?' She'd given him her best smile.

'I'd rather be on my own,' he'd said.

Instead of turning towards the high street, he'd swerved through the entrance to the park, taking one of the paths that led to the playground.

'This is a long way round,' she'd said, trying to sound jokey. She'd had to break into a jog to keep up with him. 'Jake?'

He'd stopped walking and swung round. 'Molly, go home. Please.'

Thinking about it later, she realised he'd spoken firmly but kindly. At the time, though, she'd seen it as an outright snub. She wasn't going to be brushed off like that. It wasn't as if they weren't friends, sort of. And he had kissed her. Once.

'That's not very nice, is it?' she'd said, putting her hand on his arm as he started to move again. 'We live in the same square. It's night time. You might at least let me walk with you.'

A lamp lit the path by the playground, showing Jake's face set in a grim mask, his eyes flashing fire. 'Will you just leave me alone!' And with that he'd marched off across the park and been swallowed up by the darkness of the trees.

She'd stared after him for a few seconds, then she'd run out of the park, along Albert Street and into the high street, her breathing all raggedy, her heart thumping, tears stinging her eyes.

At the time, her exchange with Jake had seemed drawn out, like a dramatic scene from a film. In truth, the whole thing had only taken a couple of minutes. But those minutes had been enough to imprint the hopelessness of the situation on her brain.

Okay, he was only some boy from the village she'd once snogged. But he wasn't *some boy*. He was Jake Harrison.

Unrequited love was the most painful feeling ever. She'd heard that, and now she knew it was true. But what was worse — if there could be anything worse — was that she'd made a complete fool of herself, following Jake when he obviously didn't want her. Demeaning herself in front of him. And now she'd never get to go out with him, because who would want to associate with a girl who behaved like that?

Having been awake all night, she was dog tired now and it was still only lunchtime. She felt so spaced out that Isla had to say her name twice before it registered properly.

'Molly, the cream tea people are coming in. Help Harry serve them, please.'

'Sure. Sorry, Isla.'

Out of the corner of her eye, she saw

Horace flick a sideways nod towards her and raise his eyes. She waited till he'd turned away again, then stuck her tongue out. A little kid at a nearby table laughed. Molly winked at him, and slipped him a marshmallow.

★ ★ ★

It wasn't Horace's night for working in The Goose and Feather — he was on tomorrow, Christmas Eve — but after he'd eaten what remained of the stew for his dinner, he nipped along to the pub for a spot of convivial cheer, and there she was again — Olive, nattering away with Valerie who owned the wool shop and her husband.

It was while he was standing at the bar that Olive caught his eye and waved him over. 'Here, sit yourself down, Horace.' She pulled up a spare chair to the table.

Feeling defeated, Horace obediently sat.

'That worked out all right today,

didn't it?' Olive beamed triumphantly. 'There I was, thinking I'd be on my own for Christmas after you turned me down, and then you comes along asking me to help out in the caff — and before I know where I am, I'm being invited to Christmas dinner, along with you!' She looked at the others. 'Looking forward to that, I am.'

'Are you?' Horace growled into his beer. 'I'm not so sure I am. Not now the world and his wife's coming along as well.'

Olive wasn't fazed. She laughed heartily. Her bosom trembled inside its casing of raspberry-pink wool. 'Hark at him! The world and his wife! I've been called many things in my time but not that. You are a card, Horace.'

'I'm sure you'll both have a lovely time,' Valerie said, smiling at the two of them.

Not long after, she and her husband got up to go, leaving Horace stranded with Olive.

'S'pose you wants a drink,' he said.

'That's very kind. I'll have another shandy. Oh no, make it a gin and tonic! It is Christmas, after all.'

'Not yet it bloomin' isn't,' Horace grumbled, getting up and pushing his way back to the bar.

As he stood there waiting to be served, he felt a nip of pain low down in his guts. Tonight's stew was weighing a bit heavy. He wondered what tender delicacy Olive had cooked up for her own dinner tonight. Not warmed-up stew, he'd place bets on that.

She'd done wonders in the café today. Funny how he hadn't thought twice about running round to her house and asking her to help out. Shot himself in the foot there, though, hadn't he? He hadn't foreseen that invitation from Isla. Still, it would have been a shame if Olive had to have her Christmas dinner on her own. He stole a glance at her. She was a handsome woman, in a low light. And those scones, they were so light they could have flown right out of the window. Perhaps it was time he cut her a bit of slack.

'Make that gin a double,' he said to the bartender.

December 24th
Christmas Eve

One day until Christmas

Yesterday, after the cream tea party had left and Molly and Harry were clearing the tables, she told him what had happened with Jake the night before. She was glad she had. He hadn't played it down, or made her feel stupid, or told her to get over it, or anything like that. He'd just listened, and then asked her if she was feeling better about it now. She'd thought about it and realised that, surprisingly, she *was* feeling better, and the scene with Jake which had seemed so incredibly embarrassing had already lost most of its drama.

Waking up this morning, she experienced a tiny flinch inside as she remembered, but that was all. Anyway, she doubted

Jake had given her another thought after she'd dashed off. She was still wondering why he'd gone into the park in the first place. It couldn't have been simply to get away from her, could it? It seemed a bit overdramatic. She still really liked him, probably would for a while, but if he didn't want to go out with her, there was nothing she could do about it. It was his loss.

Molly bounced downstairs for breakfast and found her mother on the phone.

'Jean,' she mouthed at Molly, pulling a face which made Molly pause with the cereal box in her hand.

Mum clicked the button on the phone. 'That was Auntie Jean.'

'Yep, got that. Is everything okay?'

'No, it's not. It's all off, Christmas at theirs. We're not going. They're down with the flu. Auntie Jean, Uncle Alan, your cousins, the whole lot of them. How's that for rotten luck?'

Molly felt her mouth start to stretch into a grin. She bit her lip to stop it.

'How horrible for them,' she said.

'Yes, it is. This bug that's doing the rounds is the devil to shake off.'

'So,' Molly ventured, 'what will we do for our Christmas dinner? Go to Nan's?'

Mum threw up her hands. 'It's too late for that. Nan's got all her arrangements made. No, we'll stop here. We'll be fine. Good job I'm not working today. I'll nip round the high street, see what's left. Or I could get a bus to the supermarket. There'll be more choice there.' She smiled. 'Don't worry, I'll do us a nice dinner.' She gave Molly a sideways look. 'You'll be able go to that party tonight now, the one that was so important.'

Molly shrugged. 'Might do.'

'Might do? After all that fuss you made about it? Honestly, Molly, I don't know where I am with you, I really don't.' Mum laughed. 'I don't suppose you know yourself, half the time.'

It was true; now she was free to go to Sarah's party, for some reason she'd gone off the idea. It wasn't because she didn't want to run into Jake — she just wasn't in the mood for it anymore.

She poured out her cereal and flicked the kettle on. 'Do you want another cuppa, Mum?'

'Yes, please, love.'

Her mother handed over her mug. She looked a bit downcast, Molly thought. She must have been looking forward to Christmas at Auntie Jean's. Molly felt mean now for making such a song and dance about it in the first place. Her mum must be lonely at times, even though she'd never admit it. It couldn't be easy for her, staying cheerful for Molly's sake, never letting her true feelings show.

'I'm not going to the party. I'm not leaving you on your own on Christmas Eve. We'll have a girly night in, watch a soppy film, get pizza maybe.'

Her mum's face lit up, then she fell serious. 'Honestly, love, I'll be fine. You should be out with your friends at your age, it's only right.'

'*Mum.*'

'Yes, love?'

'Don't argue. I'm staying in with you and that's final.'

Leaving the house ten minutes later, Molly found a long white envelope on the mat, addressed to her. No time to see what it was now. She stuffed it in her bag and left the house — just as Jake was coming out of his front door. Molly squared her shoulders, lifted her head and walked calmly across the square towards the high street, without acknowledging him.

⋆　⋆　⋆

Isla's mother had phoned again last night. Although she never said as much, it was obvious from her tone that she was still worrying about Isla being upset over Kate. No amount of cheeriness from Isla was ever going to convince her that she was fine — as fine as she could be, anyway. Her mother was caught in the middle, and Isla was sorry about that. Their conversations were never easy anymore. All subjects, however innocuous,

131

led eventually down the same old road, and triggered the same old questions.

Supposing Sam had made it to the wedding and they'd gone through with it? Would they have sailed along, playing the roles of the sweetly romantic couple, head-over-heels in love with each other? Fooling everybody, fooling themselves? How long would they have kept that up?

Sam's proposal had been a reflex action. He'd admitted sleeping with Kate — he'd had no choice. He'd even admitted that it had happened a couple of times, a little detail Kate had neglected to share. They'd argued and debated and made up and argued again, every day and every night, for weeks. Eventually, exhausted and claustrophobic, they'd needed to go somewhere, do something. Nottingham Castle had been Sam's suggestion. They'd stood beneath cloudy skies on a steep grassy slope, soaring walls behind them, the city laid out in miniature below, and Sam had suddenly said, 'Let's not fight anymore. Let's get married.'

It had seemed the perfect solution.

Even as she'd stepped into her dress, fixed her tiara, and been handed her bouquet, Isla had known what their engagement had meant to Sam: it was an outward sign of victory. He'd messed up, but he'd come through unscathed and wanted to let the world know. Isla had figured that being married to Sam would make her feel safe and confident and purposeful. Everything that Kate had destroyed, and let Isla destroy for herself, would be restored. But above all, she was still in love with Sam, and that was why she'd agreed to marry him. The rest would follow.

In time, she would start to feel grateful to Sam for admitting there was nothing right about the wedding, even if he had left it until the last minute, leaving her drowning in misery and humiliation. For now, she'd ride out the emotional storm, keep busy, and hope that her heart was quietly getting on with mending itself.

Harry was already making breakfast

when she came downstairs, still in her pyjamas, pale-faced and headachy from a night of shallow, fitful sleep. 'I can't do this,' she said, dropping into a chair and sneezing twice.

Harry turned from the cooker where he was poaching eggs, his expression enquiring.

'Today, tomorrow, this stupid bloody Christmas I've let us in for. All of it. I can't do it. I just can't.'

Harry's eyes softened with concern. 'You'll have me to help. I'll be with you every step of the way.'

'I don't just mean the work.'

'I know.' Harry nodded. He indicated the eggs. 'Can I tempt you?'

Isla felt immediately grateful. Harry was letting her know he understood without making a big thing of it.

'Just toast, please. And tea, if you're making it.'

He smiled. 'Coming right up.'

'Sorry, you're probably feeling as rubbish as me. This time of year, everything's kind of magnified, isn't it?'

'Yep. But actually, I'm pretty much okay today. If you want to talk, I'm sure we can play hooky for half an hour.'

Isla sighed and put her head in her hands. 'I don't even know if I want to talk. I don't seem to know anything this morning. But cheers anyway.'

'Isla . . . ' Harry gave her a long look.

She sighed. 'This Christmas would have been my first — our first — as a married couple. Sam and me. He jilted me at the altar. Well, on the church porch, technically. I thought that only happened in telly soaps, but apparently it happens in real life as well.'

'Oh Isla. I had no idea.'

'Not something you'd have guessed at, presumably.'

'God, no. I suspected a love affair gone wrong. That would have been bad enough, but not that.'

'I wouldn't have guessed about you and the baby. Life is full of shit at times, isn't it?'

Harry smiled ruefully. 'Oh yes. There's always plenty of that stuff kicking about.'

He brought his eggs on toast to the table. 'May I ask, when did this happen?'

'October the 31st.'

'Blimey, that recently? No wonder you're struggling. I'm so sorry, Isla. Now I'm even more surprised, and grateful, that you took me in when you had all that going on in your head. I mean, why bother?'

Isla laughed, her first time this morning. 'My natural curiosity came out trumps. Anyway, I had an ulterior motive, don't forget that.'

'Maggie and her broken ankle. I hadn't forgotten. You didn't have to give me a bed, though. That makes you a Good Samaritan in my book.'

'If you say so.'

Harry ate his breakfast in silence for a while. Then he said, 'Isla, you *can* do today, and you can do tomorrow, and that's because you don't have a choice. It's only two days, then it'll all be over. Well, not *all*. Our enforced Christmas, I mean. I probably shouldn't say this, but it might be a blessing in disguise for both of us. We'll be so busy making sure Horace and Olive have an edible dinner, we won't have time to sink into depression.'

'I still can't do it,' Isla said. 'My feet won't get me as far as The Ginger Cat. I'm stuck, here inside.' She tapped her temple, feeling and sounding, to her own ears, hopeless and pathetic as well as melodramatic, but she couldn't help it.

Harry got up and put his plate in the dishwasher. 'Well, let's go and do it anyway. You'd better get dressed first, though, unless you want to stop the traffic in the high street.'

Isla smiled. She felt a little better already, and that was down to Harry. She hardly knew him, but she knew enough to wonder at Claudia's stupidity. The bloke she was unfaithful with — had got pregnant by — couldn't have held a candle to Harry. Perhaps, in time, Claudia would realise what she'd lost. By then it would be too late, of course.

As it would be too late for Sam. Whatever happened, she could never go back;

she knew that now. But that didn't mean she knew how to go forward.

★　★　★

Horace and Molly arrived at the café at the same time, within minutes of Isla and Harry's arrival. Horace was carrying a string bag of vegetables and muttering to nobody in particular.

''Er at the greengrocer's has got a bloomin' cheek. Tried to tell me I was storing me veg all wrong when I told her about the last lot of spuds going soft. Like I haven't been fending for meself for years.'

Molly disappeared to the back room to take off her coat and check her hair and makeup, all of five minutes since she last checked it at home. Suddenly she let out a squeal. Isla made a *What now?* face at Harry. It was Christmas Eve. The last thing they needed was more histrionics.

Molly rushed out of the back room, waving a piece of paper and almost throwing herself upon Isla. 'I got in!

I've got a place on the hair and beauty course, starting next September!'

'Oh, Molly, that's wonderful news! Well done.'

'Brilliant,' Harry said. 'Congratulations, Molly.'

Even Horace said a gruff, 'Good fer you,' and patted Molly's arm, making her giggle.

'Can I run along to the florist's and tell my mum? She'll be dead chuffed,' Molly said. And then her face dropped. 'Oh, I just remembered. They're shut today. Mum's going on the bus to the supermarket to get our Christmas dinner. If they've got anything left.'

'Oh, but I thought you and your mum were having Christmas at your auntie's,' Isla said.

'We were, but we're not now. They've all gone down with the flu.'

'Will it be just the two of you, then?'

'Yes, just me and Mum.'

Isla looked at Harry. By the look on his face, he knew exactly what was coming next.

'Molly,' Isla said, 'you might hate this idea, and please say if you do, but how about you and your mother coming to us for Christmas dinner? Horace is coming, and his friend Olive.'

Horace emitted a spluttering sound as he banged cups about behind the counter.

Molly did a kind of jig on the spot. 'Could we really? I'd love that, and it'll be company for Mum. She spends far too much time on her own, or just with me, as it is. Thanks ever so much, Isla.'

'You'd better clear it with your mother first, though. Preferably before she gets to the supermarket. You can tell her the good news about your college place at the same time.'

Molly sped off to find her mobile phone. Seconds later, she was back.

'Mum says thank you *very* much and we'd both love to come.'

'That's good then.' Isla avoided Harry's eye and went to attend to the first customers of the day, an ancient couple who came in at least three times a week for tea and toasted tea cakes, and a chat with whoever served them.

'Yes, yes, I know.' Isla raised her eyebrows at Harry as he cornered her in the kitchen five minutes later. 'But Molly's been so upset about that damn boy, and I thought if we're taking in Charnley Acre's waifs and strays, we might as well add to the numbers.'

Harry grinned. 'Am I a waif and stray?'

'Yep.' Isla nudged him. 'I'm one as well, though.'

Harry lowered his voice. 'Are you all right, Isla?'

He meant after this morning's wobble. Harry had his own emotional problems to handle; it was so kind of him to concern himself with hers as well. But that, Isla was beginning to realise, was Harry in a nutshell.

She smiled. 'I will be. Like you said, we haven't got time to be anything *but* okay, especially now.' She indicated Molly with a sideways nod.

'True. So it's all systems go, Christmas dinner at Albert Street for six.'

'No.'

'No?'

'We'll have it here, in The Ginger Cat. It makes sense, doesn't it? It's all decorated for Christmas, we've got heaps of china and stuff, and there's a big oven, big enough to take that mammoth of a turkey.'

'Which also means number eleven Albert Street remains a festivity-free sanctuary. Great idea. I like it.'

★ ★ ★

Horace wondered if he'd given Olive the wrong idea, standing her that double gin and tonic last night. She'd stuck to him like glue for the rest of the evening, meaning that everyone in the pub must have noticed. He was sure he saw the landlord give him a wink from across the other side of the bar. All well and good, but The Goose and Feather was his place of work, as well as where he spent his entire social life. Since Maureen went, Horace had been a free spirit. He had a reputation to keep up.

Talking about free spirits, he wasn't miserly, but at the same time he hoped Olive would go back to her shandy and the occasional Guinness once Christmas was out of the way. When you relied on a pension and the paltry wages from two part-time jobs, you didn't want to go forking out for gin too often. If she turned up at the pub tonight, he'd be safe, though, as he'd be busy working.

The Ginger Cat was quietish this morning, which was a blessing, as he'd be run off his feet tonight. There'd been a bit of excitement first thing, with Molly getting the letter about her college place. And then, would you believe it, Isla had only gone and invited the girl and her mum to join in with their Christmas dinner. Still, it wasn't a bad thing. Molly was a nice enough kid and he knew her mother to say hello to in passing. She seemed a good sort. At least Olive would have more people to talk to and wouldn't be foisting all her attention on him.

He had to say he was surprised when

it turned out they'd be having their dinner in the café, not at Albert Street. A bit of a busman's holiday, that. Plus, Horace wasn't sure what Jo and Lloyd would think about this break in tradition, but he could see the point, now the party had grown. And it wouldn't be so far to walk either. Hardly any distance at all.

Yes, Horace was looking forward to this Christmas. He might even blow the cobwebs off the ironing board later and give his decent shirt the once-over. And the trousers of his suit while he was about it.

The café was closing this afternoon. They had a little rush on at lunchtime but nothing to write home about. Isla told Horace and Molly to go as soon as they'd served their last table. She and Harry would finish up.

More than likely, they wanted a bit of time together, Horace thought, chuckling to himself as he put his coat on. Strangers or not — which he'd heard they were until she'd roped him in to help out — these last couple of days you'd have been hard pressed to get a fag paper in between them. Still, they were both unattached, by the looks of it, so why not give it a go?

With this romantic thought in mind, Horace called, 'Sees you tomorrow, then,' and set off for Malt Cottage.

* * *

Harry lit the fire and flopped into an armchair. He heard the sound of rushing water from above as Isla took her shower. She'd seemed fine today, but as he knew only too well, that didn't mean much. Inside was where it counted.

He couldn't stop the image that presented itself in his head: Claudia and that oaf Steven making up a Christmas stocking for the baby's first Christmas, settling her for the night, then each sneaking off to wrap the other's surprise gifts. Claudia changing into the Janet Reger pyjamas and cashmere cardigan she liked to sit around in. Steven bringing her a glass of wine, or champagne as it was Christmas Eve. Smiling as he handed it to her.

Smug bastard.

Harry had only met Steven once, when he'd gone with Claudia to a party hosted by the company both she and Steven worked for. He hadn't taken to him. The fact that Claudia seemed to think the sun shone out of every orifice should have given him a hint. The clues were there, had he not been too naïve, too trusting, to want to find them.

That Sunday morning, they'd been getting ready for the trip to the Cotswolds when Claudia received several text messages on her mobile in quick succession. Messages she'd read but hadn't replied to. Seeing her glancing at her phone every five minutes, Harry had known she was hiding something, and he'd challenged her over it. She'd told him it was work. She'd left the public relations company by then and become a recruitment consultant — the job did not involve out of hours calls, especially not at weekends.

And then she'd become very quiet and still, just before she chucked the grenade.

'I'm so sorry,' she'd kept saying. 'I thought I loved you more, and I wanted you to be the baby's father. But the truth is you're not, and Steven is. I can't go on pretending.'

I thought I loved you more. The words had rung constantly in Harry's ears, even while he mourned the loss of a child who was never his. Claudia had, according to her skewed way of looking at it, been in love with both of them, and the balance had weighed in Harry's favour, at least for a time. How very flattering.

He hadn't asked her how long the affair with Steven had been going on because by that time the history wasn't relevant. Anyway, he knew the answer: long enough.

Harry hadn't realised Isla had come into the room until she was standing right beside his chair.

'Harry? Okay?'

He looked up at her. She'd put on a

fresh pair of jeans and the oversized grey sweater. Her hair was damp around the edges.

'You were miles away,' she said.

'I was thinking about Claudia and all of that. Driving myself mad, like you do.' He smiled.

Isla perched on the arm of the chair. 'Are you still in love with her?'

'No. It still hurts but it's nothing to do with love, not anymore. I suppose it's resentment that she put me through all that. And bitterness. I don't want to feel bitter, because that's not a good way to be, but at the moment I can't help it.'

'It'll pass,' Isla said. 'Most things do, eventually.'

Harry reached for Isla's hand and held it for a moment. 'Yes, and that's what we have to keep telling ourselves. Both of us.'

A sound broke into the ensuing silence — the sound of singing.

'Hey!' Isla jumped up and went to the window. 'Carol singers! Come and see.'

She ran to the front door, Harry following.

The procession of singers was making its way along Albert Street. They were warmly dressed in scarves, hats and boots. Some carried lanterns on poles, and all held songbooks. Harry was reminded of the scenes on old-fashioned Christmas cards.

A rendition of 'O Little Town of Bethlehem' soared into the crisp air, melodic and harmonious. Harry put his hand on Isla's shoulder. They stood on the doorstep and listened as the carol changed to 'Hark the Herald Angels Sing', and as the procession drew level with the house, Harry pulled a handful of change from his pocket and went to drop it into the collection bucket.

'We must've forgotten to put the sign in the window,' he said as they came back indoors.

'What sign?'

'The one that said 'No hawkers, no circulars, no Christmas'.'

'I'm glad we forgot,' Isla said.

'So am I.'

'Are you?'

'Not really. Are you?'

'No. I'm still full up from before.'

Before they'd left The Ginger Cat, they'd made preparations for tomorrow, counting out plates and glasses, and pushing tables together into a big square. While Isla had laid the places and put the finishing touches to the table, Harry had walked back to Albert Street and returned in the campervan with the turkey and the rest of the food and drink. They'd made room in the café fridge by moving what food they could to the freezer. Some of what was left over, like the cheese scones that couldn't be refrozen, the sausage rolls and the perishable salad items, they'd eaten.

'What shall we do, then?' Isla said. 'Watch telly?'

Harry hesitated for a moment. 'Put your coat on. We're going out.'

★　★　★

Isla fastened her seat belt. 'Where are we going?'

'I thought it was time I saw some of the landscape around here.'

'What, in the dark?'

'Best time.'

They drove along the high street and past The Goose and Feather, where revellers spilled out of the open door in a burst of light, teenagers stood about in chattering groups, and late shoppers stepped down from the Cliffhaven bus, their arms weighed down with carrier bags. Harry drove them through the village and over the crossroads, taking the turning that led up Charnley Hill. At the top of the steep incline, he pulled the van into the small parking bay, where in daylight visitors stopped to admire the view across farmland and hills, with a glimpse of the sea in the distance.

Isla had never seen the countryside looking as beautiful as it did now. Purple shadows claimed the dips between the hills and cast the fields below into soft darkness, complete apart from the squares of yellow light from cottage and farm-house windows. Above, a three-quarter moon and myriad stars transformed a deep navy-blue sky into a theatrical back-cloth.

'Breathtaking, isn't it?' Harry said.

Isla nodded. She realised her cheeks were wet.

'Don't cry. My driving wasn't that bad, was it?'

'I'm not crying, not really. It's just . . . ' She waved a hand towards the windscreen. 'All this.'

'I know.' Harry's voice was solemn. 'Gets you right where it hurts.'

They were silent for a while, then Harry spoke again.

'You asked me earlier if I was still in love with Claudia. Are you still in love with Sam?'

'There's a small part of me that will always be in love with him,' Isla said after a moment. 'Sam didn't love me. He did at the start, and then he must have stopped, otherwise he couldn't have behaved the way he did. Not only did I lose Sam, but I lost Kate, too. She was my best friend.'

'Do you mean she and Sam . . . ?'

'Yes, but there was more to it than that. When I was in my twenties, I started having negative thoughts. I felt that somehow I wasn't good enough, not clever enough or pretty enough or worthy enough. I felt inferior to everyone else. Don't ask me why I did; something must have triggered it, but I never knew what. My parents were brilliant. I got counselling, and all sorts. Nothing worked, so I found my own solution. I started drinking. I wasn't an alcoholic, never got that far; but when Kate and I went out on the town, we partied like mad because at the time everybody did. But I took it to extremes, and Kate looked after me and supported me — literally — sometimes. She used to take me to her house to sober up before I went home, so mum and dad never knew the extent of the problem. Drinking made me feel better in myself. I had confidence, and I started to feel like I was *somebody* again.'

She glanced at Harry to see what he was making of all this but his face gave nothing away.

'I tried to stop, lots of times, but I always went back because I wanted that good feeling, you know? And then one day I looked at myself in the mirror, really looked, which was something I'd been avoiding, and I saw what others must have seen. I looked dreadful. My skin was sallow, my eyes were dark pits, I had a sort of haunted look about me, and I decided there and then that I would stop drinking for good and turn my life around.'

She paused for breath. Harry waited. His quiet presence felt like a warmth, surrounding her, encouraging her.

'And I did stop. I avoided the party scene, and stopped going out altogether for a while. I had the early nights Mum was always telling me I needed. It paid off; I got a promotion at work and my life was back on track. But I missed having fun with my mates, so I started going out again, to quieter places, staying away from the hub of the nightlife. I stuck to fizzy water and soft drinks and, surprisingly, I enjoyed myself as much as I had when I'd been getting drunk, only without the aftermath.'

'You beat it on your own,' Harry said. 'That was quite an achievement. Sorry, that sounds patronising. Unintentional.'

'No, it doesn't, not at all.' She gave Harry a smile. 'And then I met Sam. I worked in events management — still do, technically — and he came to us to organise a stag do for his best mate. We got serious very fast, and saw one another almost every night. I was so happy. I loved him to bits, my parents thought he was the best thing that had happened to me, and I thought so, too.

'A few months later, Kate persuaded me to have a night out in town, like before. We went on a crawl of our old haunts, me on Cokes and orange juice, Kate drinking moderately but not pushing me to join in. We were having a laugh, and I was all over the place. I remember at one point having a wee in an alleyway, and then I must have passed out because the next thing I knew, Kate was hauling me upright and she'd got some bloke to give us a lift back to her house. I was living in the flat by then and I didn't make it home until three the next afternoon. My mother was frantic and about to call the police. She'd been trying to get in touch with me all night because I hadn't answered her messages, and Sam had no idea where I was either.'

'But how come you got in such a state?'

'Kate had spiked my drinks with vodka. She'd slipped some sort of pill in as well, for good measure. At the time I had no idea it was her or that she was even capable of such a thing. I went over and over that night in my mind, as much as I could remember of it, and eventually I decided that some blokes we'd chatted to in the first bar had been the culprits. They'd been pretty wasted and they probably thought it would be a laugh.

'Around a week after that, I was talking to a couple of girls I knew who'd been in the bar that night, and they told me what Kate had done. I refused to believe them at first, but they were deadly serious. They had no reason to make it up.'

Isla looked at Harry. 'I'm sorry, you don't want to hear my depressing tale of woe. I'll shut up now.'

'Actually, I do want to hear it. But if you want to stop, Isla, do that, and we'll go home.'

'No, I'll tell you the rest. I want to tell all of it.'

She nodded, acknowledging what a relief it felt to talk about it to somebody who was, in effect, a stranger. Somebody who wouldn't judge.

Isla continued the story. Kate, unsurprisingly, had kept clear of Isla after that night. Guilt, Isla had surmised at the time. But Isla wasn't going to let her off scot free. She'd been disciplined at work for missing an important meeting with a client that day, and almost lost her job over Kate's recklessness.

Kate agreed to meet her. They sat on a bench in a park one lunch hour and Kate had acted friendly, as if it was an ordinary meeting. But Isla saw through her.

'I know what you did,' she'd said. 'You didn't think I'd find out but I have, so you might as well own up. You tried to wreck my life when I'd just got it back together. Come *on*, Kate. The truth, please.'

And Kate had looked Isla right in the eye, held up her hands and said, 'Okay, okay. I slept with Sam. Guilty as charged.'

'Funnily enough,' Isla said, 'I never did confront her about the drink spiking — I had bigger things to deal with — but I can only think Kate was jealous. Of me with Sam, of me in general, I don't know. It doesn't make sense but that's the only explanation I can come up with.'

She told Harry about Sam's eventual proposal at Nottingham Castle, and made him laugh over the bridesmaids in black.

'The rest you know.' She looked at her watch. 'We'd better go home. We've got to be up at sparrow's cough to get that turkey in the oven. Or one of us has.' She paused. 'Harry, thank you for bringing me here. And for, you know, listening. What a pair we are.'

Harry started up the campervan. 'We are indeed.'

★　★　★

Harry squinted at his phone: it was almost two a.m. He hadn't been asleep for long; thinking about Isla's story, imagining in graphic detail what he'd like to do to Sam and Kate, had kept him awake. He thought he'd heard movement outside his room — no, *in* his room. It would be one of cats; Bentley, probably. Although this time he felt sure he'd closed the door fully.

He turned over, and saw a shape in the darkness, beside the bed.

A shape that was Isla.

'I couldn't sleep,' she whispered, as if

there was anyone else to hear.

Raising himself up on one elbow, Harry lifted the duvet. Isla slid in beside him, immediately resting her head on his shoulder. His arm went tentatively around her, and she snuggled in.

'Is this okay?' she said. 'I just wanted . . . I needed . . . '

'Sshh. I know.'

He kissed the top of her head.

Some time later, or it might not have been very long at all — for some reason he'd lost track of time — she snuggled closer, and his body automatically moulded itself to hers. After a while, she turned over in his arms and their mouths met. She broke away to shimmy out of her pyjama trousers.

'Isla, are you sure . . . ?'

The answer came in the insistence of her kiss, and the pressure of her hands as they caressed his back.

December 25th
Christmas Day

No days until Christmas

When Harry woke in the morning, he stretched, and rolled across to the empty side of the bed. And then he remembered. Springing out of bed, he padded across the landing to Isla's room and peeped in through the partially open door, half-expecting to find her curled up in a ball of misery and regret. But the room was empty, the curtains drawn wide, the bed neatly made. It was only just gone eight o'clock.

Further investigation showed that Isla was nowhere in the house. There was a mug containing tea dregs on the draining board. The cats dozed contentedly in various resting places, replete with breakfast.

Fifteen minutes later, Harry left the house, drawing in breath as the freezing air cut into his lungs. It was barely light; the trees in the park were black etchings against a chambray sky feathered with rosy clouds. The only signs of life in Albert Street were two little kids, their breath puffing out before them like smoke as they pedalled madly along the pavement on shiny new bikes while their parents kept watch from a neighbouring doorstep.

The high street was silent and deserted. His footsteps rang out on the frost-hard pavement as he hurried towards The Ginger Cat. He slowed before he reached the door, nerves skittering through him. How would it be, with Isla? Had she left the house early so that she didn't have to face him? Perhaps he shouldn't have been so eager to rush after her.

He pushed open the door of the café without giving himself any more time to think. She greeted him with a bright smile.

'You didn't have to get here so early. I

hope I didn't wake you up. I didn't mean to.'

'No, but I wish you had. We're in this together, remember?'

Harry smiled in return. The smile stuck — he couldn't seem to stop it.

Isla seemed fine, as far as he could tell. As for himself, something had changed after last night, as if a door had been unlocked, a door he'd been standing hopelessly on the outside of. Isla, in her need for comfort and human contact — it had been that, nothing more — had given him a sense of reconnection, with himself and with the world.

'About last night,' he began, feeling he should say something while unsure what came next.

Meeting his gaze, she shook her head slowly, and pressed a forefinger to her lips. Harry gave a little nod in acknowledgement.

Isla lifted a bag of vegetables from the floor onto the counter top. 'I rang my mother and she said to cook the turkey long and slow, so that's what I'm doing.

It's in already. The puds are microwave-able. The pigs are already in blankets. We just have to do the veg and the gravy. Oh, and the sage-and-onion stuffing.'

'Stuffing?'

'This.' She pointed to two boxes.

'Ah. My mother calls it seasoning.'

Isla laughed, and poked him in the chest. 'Posh boy.'

'I'm not posh.' Harry lifted his chin, feigning a miffed expression.

'Do *posh boys* know how to peel spuds?'

'Yup. They also know how to make brandy butter.'

'Oh God, I forgot about that!' Isla crossed the kitchen, opened the door to the larger store cupboard, and rooted about amongst the sundry bottles lurking in its dark depths. She finally came up with a half-bottle of brandy. 'Voila! There's all sorts in here. Lloyd's secret stash, I expect.'

'Butter we have. Icing sugar?'

'Of course. In the top cupboard.'

Harry smiled. 'Then we're good to go.'

'Happy Christmas, love.'

Molly's mum tipped a load of presents into Molly's lap as she sat curled up on the sofa in her pyjamas. On the table in front of the sofa were two empty plates, smeared with maple syrup and dotted with stray blueberries. They always had pancakes for breakfast on Christmas morning, with the *Carols from King's* DVD playing on the telly.

'Oh, Mum, all these! I've only got you two!'

Molly reached down by the side of the sofa for her mother's presents.

Mum waved a dismissive arm. 'They're only little things. I enjoyed picking them out. Been doing that since October.'

'Yeah, right.' Molly raised her eyes. October? It was probably more like August when Mum had started her Christmas shopping.

Molly's smile grew wider as she un-wrapped parcel after parcel, each one prettily wrapped in either purple or pink paper decorated with stars and snowmen. There were lip-glosses, makeup items, bath fizzers, hair clips, dark grey glittery tights — all kinds of lovely things. Lastly, she lifted the lid of a long blue velvet box. Inside was a tiny pair of open scissors on a fine silver chain.

'It's real silver, mind,' Mum said, looking a little bit teary. 'So look after it.'

'I will. I love it.' Molly held up the necklace so that the scissors swung, glinting in the light from the Christmas tree. 'Thanks ever so much, Mum.' She gave her mother a kiss on the cheek.

'I'm very proud of you for getting onto the hair and beauty course. Dad would have been, too.'

Molly nodded, and swallowed hard. 'Open your presents, then.'

Her mother unwrapped first the furry animal-print slippers, then the chunky-knit jumper in a deep plum shade.

'Gorgeous.' She held the jumper to her face. 'So soft. And slippers! I feel spoilt, lovey, I really do.'

Kissing Molly on the cheek, she got up from the sofa and picked up the empty plates. 'We'll be all right today, won't we? Having our dinner at The Ginger Cat?'

'Of course.' Molly frowned.

She couldn't think what Mum meant for a moment. And then it dawned on her that, apart from Molly, her mother would be spending Christmas with people who were virtually strangers. She knew Horace to say hello to, and possibly Olive, but Isla and Harry not at all. Mum didn't have time to sit about in The Ginger Cat; she was too busy working at the florist's.

Molly smiled up at her mother. 'It'll be great, you'll see.'

'Yes, well it was very kind of them to include us. It'll be more fun for you, too, being in a party instead of just with me.'

'No, Mum. We'd have been fine, whatever,' Molly said firmly.

When her mother had gone to the kitchen, Molly raised herself off the sofa, went to the window, and gazed across Honeypot Square towards Jake's house. She wondered what he was doing now; whether he'd had breakfast, or opened his presents. She didn't feel embarrassed anymore about chasing him across the park. It was a moment of madness, soon forgotten. The next time she bumped into him, she'd be able to talk normally without feeling awkward about it. It would be good, though, if she *did* bump into him, fairly soon. It would sort of get it out of the way.

Molly took a last, long look at Jake's house, then went upstairs to choose her outfit for the day.

* * *

Horace woke to the familiar chime of church bells calling the faithful to worship. Well, not all faithful. Hadn't he seen with his own eyes her from the flat over the butcher's, scuttling up the path of St Luke's to evensong, brazen as you like? Everyone knew she'd been carrying on

168

with the brother of the landlord of The Goose; him from Meadowside, who had a wife and four kids. Common knowledge, that was.

It had crossed Horace's mind that the unfortunate woman had gone to church to pray for forgiveness, but he'd soon dismissed that idea. It would take a lot more than a few prayers and blessings by the vicar to put her back on the straight and narrow. Oh yes.

Horace pulled the covers up to his chin and stared up at the ceiling. One of these days he'd have to see to that damp patch. Maureen had reckoned it was the same shape as India. Might've been, back then. Now it was more like India, Pakistan and half of China, he shouldn't wonder. That was the trouble with these old places. Always something needing seeing to.

He wouldn't mind betting Olive Cowstick's house was as dry as a bone and snug with it. Not that Horace would ever move from Malt Cottage; there was only one way he'd be leaving here, and that was in a box.

Olive! Horace threw back the covers and sat bolt upright, making the glass containing his teeth wobble dangerously on the nightstand. There he'd been, listening to the bells and thinking it was Sunday when, instead, it was Christmas Day! It wasn't surprising he'd forgotten. Last night, the pub had been packed to its oak beams and Horace hadn't had time to draw breath, never mind pop out for a ciggie. He'd been run off his feet, literally. When at last the place had emptied and he'd helped clear up the mess, he'd hardly been able to put one foot in front of the other as he'd staggered the few yards to his front door.

It was perishing cold this morning. He'd been in such a hurry to get to bed last night he hadn't put the little electric heater on to take the chill off the bedroom, as he usually did. He snuggled down again, pulling the covers up as far as his nose. Another few minutes wouldn't hurt. He had nothing to do this morning except walk across the road to The

Ginger Cat where his Christmas would be all laid on. Marvellous.

His thoughts meandered back to Olive. She hadn't repeated her offer to come round to Malt Cottage and give it a going over, but no doubt he'd be able to steer her back in that direction, given the right moment. Being so busy, it would be one burden lifted. He had let things go rather; he'd thought that the last time he looked in the oven. If Olive couldn't wait to get her hands on his muck, then who was he to deny her the pleasure?

With that thought in mind, Horace settled down for another little doze.

* * *

As the clock ticked round to one, Isla took a deep breath and pasted on a smile to welcome the first of their guests, Horace and Olive.

She'd watched them coming across the road, Olive's arm linked tightly through Horace's as if now she'd got

171

hold of him, she wasn't letting go. At least Horace opened the café door for her, holding it back to let Olive in first.

'Dunno why you needed to call for me,' Isla heard him grumble. 'I could hardly go astray in that distance, could I?'

Olive just beamed, and handed Isla a large square cake tin with a farmyard scene on the lid.

'Mince pies. I expect you've got 'em, but I was at a loose end this morning, so I thought I'd fill me time baking.'

Isla took the lid off the tin. 'As it happens, Olive, I didn't get mince pies, not proper ones like this, only some little tart things with fruit in them which aren't the same at all. These look wonderful. Thank you.'

The aroma of freshly baked pastry and dried fruit floated up, causing Horace to glance in the tin and sniff appreciatively.

''Appy Christmas,' he muttered, thrusting a carrier bag into Isla's hands.

She peered inside to find Horace's

promised contributions of a box of chocolate-covered mints and a bottle of sherry.

'Happy Christmas, Horace,' Isla said. 'I'll pour us some now, shall I? That'll be a good start.'

Harry appeared from the kitchen, red in the face and the cuff of his rolled-up shirt sleeve splashed with what looked like gravy. 'Merry Christmas, all.' He took the bottle of sherry from Isla. 'I'll do the honours. It'll have to be wine glasses, but we can wash them out afterwards for the wine.'

Horace grinned toothily. 'Shouldn't bother. It all goes down the same 'ole.'

Molly and her mother arrived a few minutes later. 'This is Mum,' Molly said unnecessarily, as they all stood round in a slightly awkward group.

'Sandra,' Molly's mother said, blushing a bit. 'Very pleased to meet you. Properly I mean, not just in passing. It was very kind of you to invite us.'

She smiled, and Isla saw how alike mother and daughter were. Molly gave a slow shake of her head, as if her mother's formality had embarrassed her.

Sandra handed Isla a bottle of white wine in a holly-patterned bag. 'Our little contribution.'

'There were meant to be chocolates as well,' Molly said, 'but I opened them last night. I didn't know they were special for today. Soz.'

'I'll *soz* you in a minute.' Sandra grinned, and poked her daughter in the arm.

'Well, thanks for the wine.' Isla said, 'It's lovely to have you. Have a sherry — there's some poured out. If you'll excuse me, I'll just pop back to the kitchen.'

Harry had beaten her to it. Isla closed the door behind her. 'They're all dressed up! I should have brought a dress to change into.' She glanced down at her jeans and T-shirt.

Olive's ample frame had been squeezed into a black woollen dress, festooned with several ropes of pearls. Miniature Christmas trees dangled from her ears. Horace was wearing a navy-blue suit clearly dating from a time when he was several sizes larger, with a brown and white striped shirt and a green tie. He smelt faintly of mothballs. Molly was in black leggings and a sparkly tunic top. A shower of silver stars sprang from the band of her ponytail. Sandra wore a fitted red dress with a black patent belt. Her hair, the same blonde shade as Molly's, was folded into a neat French pleat.

'You're fine as you are,' Harry said. 'I'm in jeans, aren't I? It's not a dressy-up time, Christmas Day.'

'Isn't it? No, you're right. I would have worn jeans at home if I'd been there for Christmas.' Isla peeled away the layers of tea towels which had been keeping the turkey hot and picked up the carving knife and fork. 'Let's get this show on the road. I tell you something, I've got new respect for my mother. It's bloody exhausting, cooking a Christmas dinner. And that's official.'

★　★　★

Harry caught Isla's eye across the table and gave her a fleeting smile. She widened her eyes at him in return. Around them, everyone seemed to be talking at once. Horace was telling a story about some long-ago Christmas, the same story that had been going on for the last ten minutes with no visible end point. Olive was nodding at random, half listening but interjecting with memories of her own. Sandra and Molly were happily arguing the merits of *Strictly Come Dancing* versus *Dancing on Ice*. The dinner plates had been cleared away, while the pudding plates remained. Nobody seemed to want to move.

Harry was just wondering if he should open another bottle of wine when Horace finally stopped telling his story, leaned back from the table and patted his stomach.

'That was a top-class dinner. You two deserves a medal.'

'We does,' Harry said, nodding. 'I mean, we do.'

Isla giggled. 'Coffee, anyone? We've

got it on tap so we might as well.'

'I'll make it.' Molly got up from the table.

'Don't suppose you could run to a nice cup of tea?' Olive said. 'And the same for Horace.'

'I can speak for meself. How d'you know what I want?'

'Which is it then, Horace?' Molly said. 'Tea or coffee?'

'Tea. Please.'

Isla fetched a plate of Olive's mince pies and put it in the centre of the table, along with the mint chocolates Horace had brought.

His mug of tea and two mince pies in front of him, Horace leaned across to gaze at the coffees Molly had served. 'I see you've not mastered the stars yet. They still looks like dogs' turds.'

'Ooh, look at these,' Olive said suddenly, obviously in an attempt to divert everyone's attention from Horace's comment. She reached out to the Christmas tree.

'If I'm not mistaken, these balls are

the originals. We had 'em in the fifties. Came from Woolworth's, as I remember.'

Everybody looked. The baubles Olive was admiring were painted with flower designs.

'Jo told me most of the decorations on the tree were vintage,' Isla said. 'Lovely, aren't they?'

Olive let the bauble swing back into place. 'You don't often see those now. Nobody keeps the old stuff. All thrown out and modern ones got in.'

'I've still got 'em, same as that,' Horace said, looking indignant. 'And the tree, same age.'

Olive gave him a fond look. 'Now, why doesn't that surprise me?'

'Right,' Horace said, smacking both hands on the table, 'you know what we need now?'

Harry smiled enquiringly. 'What's that, Horace?'

Whatever Horace wanted, he could have, and it wasn't just the wine talking. He'd got through Christmas — well, almost. He hadn't thought about Claudia or the baby all day, except in a distant, non-involved kind of way. But what pleased him more than anything was to see Isla truly smile, in a way that she hadn't since he'd met her.

Was that really only five days ago?

Horace was speaking. Harry snapped his attention back.

'A nice game of rummy. Always goes down well after the dinner.'

'Ooh, we know how to play rummy, don't we, Moll?' Sandra said. 'You remember Nan teaching you?'

'I don't think we've got playing cards.' Harry looked at Isla, who shook her head.

'No matter.' Horace was up from the table. 'I'll nip across the road and get mine.'

'I bet those'll be marked,' Olive said as the door closed on Horace, who'd gone out still wearing the red paper crown he'd got in his cracker.

Isla nodded towards Harry to follow her to the kitchen. 'When are they going home?' she whispered, then burst into giggles.

'Sometime never, I expect,' Harry said. 'Do you mind?'

'No, actually, I don't. If they're enjoying themselves, let them stay. I'm going to nip home and feed the cats. I'll take them some turkey.'

'I'll go if you like.'

'I'm fine. I could do with the fresh air. You play rummy with the others.'

'Can I cheat? I always cheat at cards.'

'No!' Isla was still laughing as she fetched her coat.

★ ★ ★

Molly stole a glance at her mother, who was concentrating hard on the hand of cards she'd been dealt, her lips pressed together. She'd really enjoyed herself today, and that was so good to see. Molly had been truthful when she'd said the two of them would have been fine at home on their own, but this was so much nicer.

She had wondered if it would feel strange having Christmas dinner where she worked, but it hadn't at all. The café was warm and cosy, and she'd had time to look properly at the pretty tree and all the decorations Jo and Lloyd had put up instead of running past them when she was serving customers. Olive had got everybody talking, even Mum, who could be a bit shy at times, and Harry had made them all laugh by reading out the jokes from the crackers in funny voices.

Molly had been surprised to find out he was the new vet in the village — she hadn't seen that coming. Horace definitely hadn't. He'd said 'Well, I'll be blowed' about a hundred times. It obviously wasn't a surprise to Isla, though.

Molly had dropped out of rummy after they'd played twice, and Isla had taken her place when she'd come back from feeding the cats. Now Molly was sitting back, playing around on her phone and feeling sleepy from all the lovely food and the glass of wine Mum had allowed her to have.

It was nearly dark outside now. The high street looked completely different with the shops all shut up and hardly anyone walking by. Like it did at night, only more peaceful, somehow. Somebody was walking by now, across the other side of the road. Molly's heart jumped. It was Jake! He stopped to take something out of his coat pocket — chewing gum, by the looks of it. As he popped a piece into his mouth, he glanced across at The Ginger Cat, and instead of walking on, he stood on the pavement with his hands in his pockets, still looking. Whether or not he could see her through the steamed-up window she couldn't tell, but there was only one way to find out.

'Hey, Mollykins!' He greeted her with such a lovely smile that her heart almost turned inside out and any leftover crumb of embarrassment was swept away. If anyone else had called her Mollykins, she'd have clocked them one. But not when it was Jake.

'I thought it was you. What's that all about then?' He nodded towards The Ginger Cat.

Molly explained.

'Funny sort of Christmas,' Jake said.

'I s'pose it is. Why are you out? Are you going somewhere?'

She gave herself a mental slap. Why did these stupid questions pop out of her mouth every time she was with Jake?

'I fancied some fresh air. It's stuffy indoors.'

Jake looked away, taking the gum out of his mouth, squidging it into a ball and flicking it into the gutter. And then Molly remembered their chat in Honeypot Square, when Jake had said his Christmas had gone a bit skywards. She had never found out what he meant — well, of course she hadn't.

She took a deep breath. 'Is it all right, Christmas at your house? I mean, are you having a good time and everything?'

Jake didn't answer at once. He looked

down at the bit of gum in the gutter, then back at Molly. 'It's perishing out here. You've got no coat.'

Molly shrugged. 'It's back there.' She pointed across the road.

'Why don't you fetch it and walk with me? Not far, just up the road and back.'

★ ★ ★

They walked to the end of the high street, as far as the row of small cottages tacked onto the end, before the cross-roads. Jake hardly spoke on the way, so Molly didn't either. But it felt okay, not awkward or anything.

Jake sat down on a wall between two of the cottages. There were lighted Christmas trees in the front windows of both; they looked so pretty. Molly said so. Jake turned to look, then smiled at Molly and patted the wall next to him. She sat down, wondering what was next.

'My father came home yesterday,' Jake said in a voice that made it sound as if it was something important.

'Home from where?'

'Back in the summer he moved out to live with a new woman. His *girlfriend*.' He spat the word out. 'My mother made him choose, and he chose her. It broke Mum's heart.'

'Your dad had an affair?' Well, obviously. But she couldn't think what else to say.

'Yep. My mother had suspected all along. My brother and I knew there was something funny going on because of the way Dad had been acting — different, somehow — but we had no idea what it was until July when he packed his bags, and Mum told us.'

Molly must have looked shocked; at least, she felt it.

Jake shrugged and smiled. 'These things happen. You just never think they're going to happen to you.'

'No, you don't.' Molly shook her head, thinking of her own father.

'Anyway, to cut a long story short, my daft 'aporth of a dad reckoned he knew he'd made a mistake as soon as he'd left us, only he was too proud to say so. Until about a month ago when he asked to see Mum. She went out one night, dressed up like she was going on a date. It turned out she'd gone to meet my father.'

Molly nodded knowingly. 'She would have wanted to look her best to show him what he'd been missing. That's what I would have done.'

Jake chuckled in a nice way, not in a making-fun way. His arm crept around her shoulders, as if he wasn't sure she'd like it.

She liked it. A lot.

'The story finally ended yesterday when my dad came home in time for Christmas. I'd put everything on hold while it was all going on — everything. I just wanted to be left alone. Now I feel like I've been restarted with jump-leads.' He paused, turning to give Molly a long, meaningful look. 'I've got a lot of making up to do.'

Molly's heart flickered. She ignored

it. Hearts could make mistakes.

'I like a story with a happy ending,' she said. 'I'm ever so pleased it's all sorted out.'

'Let's just say it's all good so far. Up until yesterday, when the taxi pulled up at ours and Dad got out with all his stuff, I didn't dare believe it was going to happen. But it did, and it's been like . . . normal, you know? This Christmas has been the same as last year, the same as all the years, as if he'd never been away.' Jake raised his eyes. 'I hope it lasts.'

'Oh, Jake, so do I! I'd wouldn't want you to be unhappy. That would be awful.' Well, she would hate Jake to be miserable. It was true, so why not be honest?

'That's sweet of you,' Jake said. 'Typical Mollykins.'

And before she could josh with him for calling her that, he was kissing her.

Kissing her like before. Only better. Because this time he was kissing her as if he really meant it.

'Good do, weren't it?'

'Wonderful do.' Olive clutched Horace's arm even tighter as they crossed the road, which was entirely empty of traffic. 'What was that all about then? Young Molly shooting off like an arrow from a bow and coming back seconds after to fetch her coat?'

'Weren't you listening? She'd spotted some boy walking by, Sandra said. Some 'erbert she was keen on. I reckon that's the same one she's been mooning over all week.'

'Aw, the little love. I remember what it was like at that age, don't you?'

'No, I don't,' Horace said. 'I was too busy earning a wage to get tangled up in that sort of caper.'

Olive chuckled. 'I don't believe you. Handsome lad like you must've been.'

'Believes what you like. We're here now.'

They were at the door of Malt Cottage. Olive let go of Horace's arm.

'Aren't you going to ask me in, round off the day with a nice cup of tea?'

'Could do, I s'pose.' Horace grumpily stuck his key in the lock. 'A quick one, mind. I'm looking forward to a kip.'

She was looking at his sink again, Horace realised, as Olive closed in on him while he was filling the kettle.

'We'll make it every Monday morning for definite, then, shall we? When I come round and give this place a going over?'

Horace blew out air. Had he agreed to that? If so, the wine must have gone to his head.

'We'll see.' He angled the teapot to hide its blackened inside from Olive.

'That's it, then. All settled! I'll start in the new year, and I want no talk about payment. It'll be my pleasure. You can stand me a couple in The Goose. You'd better get me a key cut, in case I arrive when you're at the café.'

He was lost, Horace thought, reaching for the biscuit tin.

Lost. Sunk. Done for. Scuppered.

Good and proper.

Funnily enough, he didn't seem to mind.

★   ★   ★

Isla and Harry sat amongst the detritus in The Ginger Cat. They'd already decided to leave the clearing up until the morning. The café would be closed for a couple of days; there'd be plenty of time for Isla to get everything ready for re-opening.

Harry positioned a second chair so that he could put his feet up on it. 'Did we just do that?'

'Do what?'

'Christmas.'

'I think that was us, yes.'

'Who'd have thought?'

Harry chuckled. 'Olive never gives up, does she? Did you see the way she was looking after Horace, passing him this and that, popping some of her potatoes on his plate? Like there weren't plenty in the dish if he'd wanted them.'

'I know. They are funny, those two.' Isla laughed. 'Horace revels in the attention, even though he pretends he doesn't. Sandra was lovely, wasn't she? Molly told me when were out in the kitchen that she's going to get her mum into internet dating in the new year.'

'Best of luck with that, then.'

'Quite. Our Molly's got ambitions, and she doesn't want her mother to be on her own when she leaves the village. When she's finished her course, she wants to go to London and become a hairdresser to the rich and famous.'

'Not any old hairdresser, then. Good for her. What about that boy?'

'Yeah, that was nice, her coming back with a date under her belt. But that's for now. She's looking to the future, and that's great.'

'Molly's following her dream.' Harry gazed at the Christmas tree, a faraway look in his eyes.

Isla kicked the chair on which Harry's feet rested. 'Listen to you, getting all maudlin.'

Harry grinned. 'That's what you have to do, though, isn't it? Keep looking forward, taking it one step at a time.'

'Are you ready to do that?'

'Yes, I think I am. I've already started, in here.' He tapped his temple. 'In a day or two I'll go back to Oxford — I've got to return the campervan and collect my car anyway. While I'm there I'll tie up a few loose ends, including getting my half of the deposit back on the house I rented with Claudia. I've done nothing about that yet. I just walked away.'

'Practicalities,' Isla said. 'They can be a saviour at times.'

'And you?' Harry said carefully. 'Any plans?'

'Me? I'll carry on here until the end of January, when my aunt and uncle will be home. Then I suppose I'll go back to Nottingham. I was on temporary contracts with the events management company; there'll be work there if I want it. And there are things I need to sort out, the same as you. I'm giving up my flat. It doesn't particularly bother me that Kate lives in the same block. I was horrified when my mother told me, but I can't run away from everyone and everything all the time. I just don't want to live there anymore.'

The flat was to have been their home after the wedding. Sam had spent a lot of time there beforehand but had never quite made the move properly. It should have been a warning. Perhaps it was, and she'd chosen to ignore it. Until just now, she hadn't been sure about giving up the flat, but it felt natural saying it aloud. It was the right thing to do. Make a fresh start, as Harry was.

'I'm not even sure I want to stay in Nottingham, but I expect I'll know once I'm back.' She paused. 'It's not running away, it's being kind to ourselves. We aren't running away, either of us. We're running *to* something else. You've got your new job and your new home. I've got . . . well, I haven't worked that out yet. But whatever it is, it will be good.'

They sat in silence for a while,

embroiled in their own thoughts. And then Harry got up and switched off the Christmas tree lights, and the fairy lights round the shelves. And shortly after that, they locked up The Ginger Cat café and walked, arm in arm, back to Albert Street.